Also by F. Sionil José

Short Stories

THE GOD STEALER AND OTHER STORIES
WAYWAYA: ELEVEN FILIPINO SHORT STORIES
PLATINUM: TEN FILIPINO STORIES
OLVIDON AND OTHER SHORT STORIES

Novellas

THREE FILIPINO WOMEN

Novels

PO-ON
TREE
MY BROTHER, MY EXECUTIONER
THE PRETENDERS
MASS
VIAJERO
ERMITA
GAGAMBA

Verse

QUESTIONS

SINS

SINS

A NOVEL

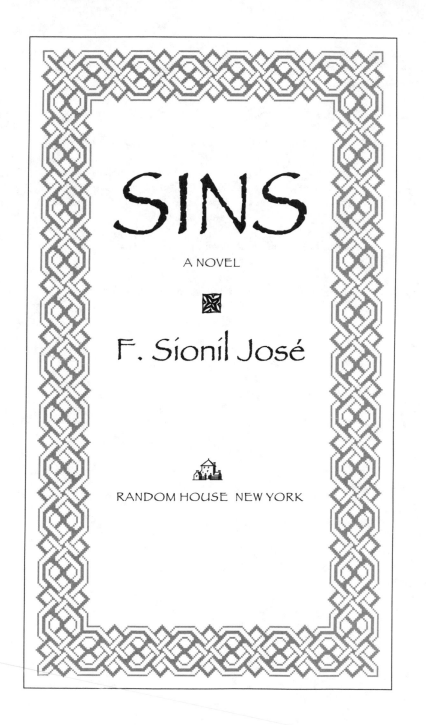

F. Sionil José

RANDOM HOUSE NEW YORK

Library of Congress Cataloging-in-Publication data is available.
ISBN 0-679-42018-5

Printed in the United States of America on acid-free paper
24689753
First Edition

Book design by Lilly Langotsky

FOR EDWIN THUMBOO

A NOTE TO THE READER

This novel contains a few words—some Spanish, some specific to the Philippines—that may be unfamiliar to the reader. A glossary has been included at the end of the book.

SINS

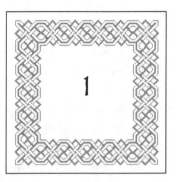

1

M y name is Carlos Cobello. My very close friends and associates call me C.C. If I were to describe myself, I would say I am what the ancient Greeks called *Anar Spoudogeloios*—a calm, collected individual, not aloof, not hottempered, serious of visage and cheerful. I have served in my country's foreign service; those who know this address me as Mr. Ambassador. As a leading member of the sugar bloc, I have, of course, been called a sugar baron. I have also been called a nationalist entrepreneur—a sobriquet I carefully nurtured and like very much. But my enemies—businessmen as well as ideologues—regard me as a predatory menace to Philippine society.

How do I begin this litany? Is this the time to do it? In my present mood of isolation and decay, crippled as I am, should I even try to put things down? A form of expiation, perhaps, or atonement, the recitation of a thousand mea culpas? And if I do it, which I know I must, should I be a slave to the rigid chronology of time or to some human conceit that will blot out everything self-deprecating? I know I have lived an interesting life, but will it be possible for me to relate this life interestingly?

Maybe I should begin by saying that I am dying—that is the most melodramatic way of starting it. They say that truth always sits on the lips of dying men. Crap! Hard-core liars lie to their last gasp, molding with apparent sincerity those fictions that they hope they can leave behind to gild, to veneer their lives of shame. I will not do this because, in truth, I have rarely lied in my life. Those who know me well, my dear Corito, my Angela, they can vouch not just for my honesty but also for my congenital decency.

I read *Hamlet* during the war and I have always believed:

> *This, above all, to thine own self be true;*
> *And it must follow, as the night the day,*
> *Thou canst not then be false to any man.*

I agree completely. *Never a lender be.* Just borrow and borrow and borrow . . .

I have always known that I will not be able to take with me anything of the vestiges of power, the artifacts and the perks of affluence that I have amassed. History tells me Alexander the Great was buried with his hands outstretched and empty to show the world, half of which was then his dominion, that he could take not even a lump of soil with him. And so it is with me. What then can I truly keep? Not my hundred antique cars now rusting away in a field in Bulacan, not the millions in jewelry I have given Angela, Corito and my women. I always replied when asked what I amassed: what else but those ineffable memories that light up the dark recesses of the past. Memories, indeed, shining now like diamonds as I pick them up one by one to polish and to caress.

But Delfin—my son, my only son in whom reposes all my

hopes, who bears in his tissues my primal genes—does not love me. Maybe, he hates me in a manner never explicit, engendered in his innermost core by his mother. Oh, Severina, forgive me. I was so young then, just as you were young, too. I loved and sinned. Forgive me.

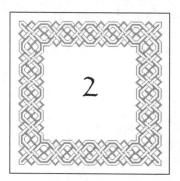

2

Now, the intractable chronology of time.

I always knew we were rich. We had this big house in Sta. Mesa, built by my grandfather when that place was wilderness, an expanse of cogon waste as my father remembered it. My grandfather, who was one of the leaders of the revolution against Spain, had the title to this land, some twenty hectares or more, which was lorded over by a low hill overlooking Manila as it was then, just a huddle of wooden houses except for the Walled City, where, for some centuries, the Spaniards had continually built houses of stone and the walls that surrounded the city. My grandfather planted the acacia trees along the street that led to the house and around the house itself, the trees that were already tall when I was a child, now great green giants that shade the street and the grounds.

My grandfather is regarded in school textbooks as a hero, and a long street that leads from Grace Park to the heart of Manila—Quiapo, that is—is named after him. By the turn of the century, he already foresaw the frenetic bustle that would bloat the city. In a sense, the old house became his formidable retreat. With its thick brick walls, its tile roof and the finest hardwood for beams and floors, it could easily last another hundred years, perhaps longer than the stone houses in Intramuros, had they not been destroyed during the war.

We had a lot of servants including Ah Chee, the amah from Canton who took care of me and my sister, Corito, four years older than I. Most of the servants came from our Hacienda Esperanza in San Quentin, Nueva Ecija. Esperanza was my grandmother's name.

I took this surfeit of ease for granted, this life of privilege to which I was born, and could hardly imagine an existence such as that of our house help and of the tenants in the hacienda with their small thatched houses. I could not see myself toiling in the fields in all that heat or slashing rain. But early on, I knew the value of money—this my mother constantly dinned into us. The price of a *ganta* of rice, of a kilo of pork; she was not poor but her family made its fortune through labor—they made furniture—not from inheritance as was my father's case. Once, Father, who early on had begun collecting Chinese porcelain, dropped a Sung vase as he was taking it from its shelf.

"It would take Jacobo," Mother said, referring to one of the drivers, "ten years of continuous work to pay for that vase." When we were eating, she would point to some particular fish—she did the marketing in Quiapo—saying that such and such fish cost so much.

I went to the San Juan de Letran College in Intramuros all through grade school. My parents spoke Spanish at home and so did my sister and I, and our amah, too. Letran was run by Spanish Dominicans and my father had friends among them. He was not going to let me grow Americanized like the boys the American Jesuits were raising at the Ateneo; to him, all the good things about this country were brought by Spain. But, like my grandfather, he was pragmatic enough to learn English, to be at home with it, for he knew it was the language of government, of business and of culture. It must be obvious from this recitation that we are mestizos, and can easily trace our pristine origins to Castille.

On this subject of our Spanish heritage, Father and I had passionate discussions. My reading of our history had broadened and, in some instances, citing chapter and verse, I would recall the clichés about friar abuses. Always, he would fall back on his last retort, that my ancestry included some friars indeed. Some of our relatives were still very much alive in Spain; I could always return and claim kinship with them. Why, then, did Grandfather join the revolution? He would smile slyly and say that if his father had not, we wouldn't be where we are today.

Like my grandfather, Father endowed his ancestry with superior intelligence, an attitude I came to share soon enough. "Oye," he used to remind me when he was running everything himself after Grandfather had died. "Look at all these native attempts at business, these Indio corporations—no sooner do they start then they fall apart. It's the corruption, the lassitude and laziness in Malay genes that enfeeble the Indios. But not those with Spanish or Chinese blood. They are the hope of this country."

Whatever one might say about him, like me, Father was concerned and regarded himself a citizen of this country.

When he talked in this manner I would be silenced; I look around me, even now, and see the shameful rubble of enterprises that the Indios, in their *ningas cogon,* so enthusiastically set up, and then destroyed.

"And it will always be this way," Father would conclude, his eyes raised to the ceiling, to a chandelier, to the fine narra beams, whatever there was for the eyes to latch onto, "because these natives are like children, just as the Spanish friars found them to be—simpleminded, incapable of intellectual or creative enterprise. The Malay in them is easily seduced by pleasure, by fiestas, by lazy habits and comfort. . . . Just watch even the poorest of them, how they while away time doing nothing. Nothing!"

Years afterward, remembering these conversations, I would analyze them; Father's arguments were awry. He always spoke as if he knew how it is to work, but he had never really worked. He did not even finish college at San Juan de Letran. To him, work was simply supervising the hacienda in Nueva Ecija, twenty thousand hectares of it, encompassing all of San Quentin and two adjacent towns. Fifteen thousand hectares were planted to sugar cane, the rest to rice. A sugar mill in the next town served our hacienda and the adjacent haciendas that were also planted to sugar. He had very good *encargados*. Father stayed in the city most of the time, attending dinners at the Club Filipino. In Manila, about a dozen clerks collected the rents from the *accesorias* and other buildings that he owned in Quiapo, Sta. Cruz and Sampaloc.

I remember him now in his prime, in his white alpaca suit and blue polka dot bow tie always, his bald head a shiny pink when exposed to the sun, an unlighted cigar in his mouth, his bushy eyebrows twitching when he spoke, his oily, bulbous nose and a receding chin much like my grandfather's. Father was short and fat—all that two hundred pounds of hulk—but he moved with litheness and grace. In his later years he always carried a silver-handled ebony cane—to ward off the dogs in the neighborhood, he always said, but he used it more on his peons who were slow to move.

I have not really described the house in all its opulence. It stands in the middle of a wide lot, on two hectares, atop this low hill. The rest of the property was subdivided into residential lots that were sold and developed in later years. In the thirties, the place seemed so far away from Manila, positioned as if it were some medieval fort. At the time, the rich mestizo families that used to live in Intramuros had already moved to the less crowded suburbs of Ermita and Malate and even farther, to Pasay and Sta. Mesa.

My grandfather, attuned to the future, bought many parcels of land adjacent to the hacienda and outside the city, toward the hills of Marikina, Makati, fields planted then to *kangkong*, and fallow land covered with worthless cogon. But the Sta. Mesa lot was his pride. It was walled with adobe, ten feet high, quarried from the vicinity. All of it was soon covered with ivy, which grew lush like bushes above the walls. The main gate, as high as the walls, was made of solid molave and braced with iron filigree, with a small entrance for people. The gatekeeper, who also helped in maintaining the garden, lived in a shed by the gate, his children part of the household staff. The garage, which could hold ten cars, was at the west end, its second floor the quarters of the five drivers, two of them bachelors. The maids and the cook slept in the wide room adjoining the kitchen. The amah, whom Mother trusted most, had a room of her own on the ground floor beside the stairs, where she could be summoned at once if needed.

The ground floor, consisting of a receiving hall paneled with narra, opened to a wide marble patio adjoining a dining hall. Beyond the patio was the swimming pool. Six bedrooms were upstairs, high-ceilinged, with ceiling fans. Their height was maintained when the entire house was provided with central air-conditioning in the fifties. Mother did not like it—she preferred fans—but Father wanted it that way for his guests.

My room faced the east, the Sierra Madre. As a boy I used to look down on terraced rice fields that were soon to become housing developments. Corito's room next to mine had the same view. My parents' bedroom across the hall overlooked Manila, as did the wide balcony where smaller parties were often held, primarily because, from there, especially at night, Manila spread out like a huge carpet studded with jewels.

Mother was four inches taller than my father, but she made no effort to look short. She wore high heels, and when walking with Father she was regal, erect but always sedate, demure, for, in truth, she never towered over him except in the management of the house, her indisputable domain, the huge garden particularly, and the kitchen.

She was a fastidious cook and a meticulous host. She did the marketing herself, assuring us of the freshest meats and vegetables. She never hired a caterer, and even when a hundred guests were expected, although she had cooks and waiters from the Manila Hotel to help, she never let go of the personal supervision, the wine list, the flowers and the table settings. She could have easily managed a five-star establishment.

I remember best the smaller dinners on the patio. She would be in the kitchen the whole afternoon, and through all that bustle, her frequent "*puñetas,*" hissing like a rocket, then the explosion of a hard slap, and the murmured, "Yes, Señora."

They came in tuxedos, the women in Valera gowns, unable to deny Mother's imperial RSVP, knowing that if they did not come without an acceptable excuse, they would forever be cut off from her list. They could ill afford this, for Mother was Manila's social arbiter, her parties attended by the country's leaders, and every visiting fireman of distinction.

So there they were, the chosen, seated at tables on the patio, candles glimmering softly, the cloying smell of dama de noche and kamuning hovering over the cool night air, and close to the ledge, before the swimming pool glazed with light, a string ensemble playing Mozart, native *kundimans* or whatever tune a guest requested. The talk was always subdued, punctuated every so often by the crack of Father's laughter. The comfort of the guests was Mother's first concern and to each table were assigned two maids in starched whites, barefoot, their hands encased in white gloves, ready to pour water, wine, into each emptied goblet. As for those pesky mosquitoes waiting to feast on exposed legs, underneath each table, hidden by lengths of embroidered linen tablecloths, were two maids squatting on the marble floor and swinging fans.

I was then in grade school. I had watched some of those parties, the garrulous poker sessions with men like President Quezon. They would play sometimes till morning, when they would be served breakfast. In the meantime, they were sustained by Carlos Primero brandy and deep-fried squid, shrimp, *chitcharon,* English biscuits with a spread of caviar or camembert. It was the *chitcharon* that I liked best, dipped in vinegar with salt, crushed garlic and powdered pepper. I would wander around the tables listening to bits of conversation, which often concerned the state; the prices of sugar, copra and gold; the horse-trading in Congress and the coming war with Japan. Like my father, they were ordinary men, bragging about their women, burping, cursing, getting drunker and drunker as dawn started to limn the east. They threw their vomit on the marble floor and dirtied the bathroom with their urine. I knew someday I would be like them.

It was only afterward, after the war, that I realized those were not simple poker sessions but meetings—or were they conspiracies?—of like minds, the division of spoils like the partitioning of Quezon City among mestizo friends. As for Quezon, he always won at those sessions, whether through collusion, skill or a mutual understanding among those who played that this was one way the leader could be thanked. I leave this for you to decide.

My father kept a kennel, six huge Dobermans that consumed more meat than we did. They were in the kennel in the daytime, but at night they were let loose in the yard to discourage any interloper. We were awakened one night; all the dogs were yammering and when the yard lights were switched on, the dogs were reaching up one of the guava trees where a frightened man was clinging, his leg bleeding. He turned out to be no thief but a very silly and daring suitor who was courting one of the maids.

Father was amused; the dogs had proven their worth, but what about this man who climbed the wall and braved injury, perhaps even death, for a woman? The intrepid act touched my father, and as soon as the man's leg had healed, Father saw to it that marriage was his reward. He was the godfather.

My boyhood brimmed with excitement. We motored then quite often to San Quentin, sometimes in the Packard with its canvas roof down. I would go horseback riding with Corito, accompanied by the *encargado*. We would gallop through the humdrum villages, sending the children scampering to safety behind the fences. Father said I had physical courage; he had seen me ride at full gallop even though early on I had fallen twice.

In truth, I was not all that brave. Sometimes, the sepulchral stillness in the house frightened me as I imagined ghosts lurking in those empty rooms. The thunderstorms at the start of the rainy season always seemed to be malignant forebodings of dark disasters. I also never liked the explosion of firecrackers in the New Year, when all the help gathered in the yard, beating cans and adding to the din. Once, Father took me heron-hunting in the green fields of San Quentin. I was perhaps twelve at the time, and big for my age. He let me aim the *escopeta*—a double-barreled, twelve-gauge Spanish shotgun. The explosion almost hurled me to the dew-washed ground, and the ringing in my ears continued the whole day. But Father was very pleased—I had aimed at a flight and had knocked down five.

During such fearsome times I rushed to Corito's room; instinctively, I knew I could not go to my parents' room and cuddle up to them—I was no longer a child. But Corito, older than I and already a young woman, was very understanding; she would let me under the covers when it was cold, hug me to quiet the tumult in my breast and laugh softly at my fears. I felt so safe with her, reveling as I did in her warmth and that delicious fragrance she exuded.

When the war came, there was not much change in our lives, but I do retain a very vivid memory of that first year we were occupied. Father had taken a very high position in the puppet government; a sign in Japanese was posted at the gate—I don't know what it meant, but I am sure it protected us from them.

Early afternoon, I was in Corito's room and we were playing chess, classes having been suspended since December when the Japanese started the war. They had occupied the school-house way below, across the cogon waste. We could see them from our windows. The noise brought Corito and me to the window.

They had lined six men against the concrete wall of the school and were executing them one by one; we could see them totter and fall after each volley. I was trembling all through those few minutes, and when we told the maids what we saw, they couldn't believe it. We told Father and Mother when they returned from some meeting early in the evening. Father said it was war, life was cheap, but we were very safe.

I was a freshman in high school, maybe thirteen or fourteen, but, as I said, already grown up physically although still juvenile in my attitudes and fears. It was not only during thunderstorms that I went to Corito—it was also when I felt so alone. She was very active socially, but after the start of the war the number of parties diminished. I remember that evening well; the last week of May and the first rain that came was accompanied by a thunderstorm. We had just finished dinner, Father was with some politicians at a meeting with the Japanese and Mother had gone to Ermita to play mah-jongg. I jumped into Corito's bed—she was reading, and she continued doing so while I hugged her. Her nightgown was open at the front, and my face was buried in her fragrant bosom, my mouth on her breast. For a while I just hugged her, comforted by the warmth of her body, her wonderful smell. I realized soon enough that my mouth was over her nipple. I started to suck it.

By the time the thunderstorm was over, I was no longer a virgin. She told me it was her first time, too. I believed her. At that age, I didn't know the difference. I suppose I was much too young to notice if my entry was obstructed—I was simply too engrossed with the senses that were pleasurably awakened in me. Corito and I never discussed this technicality again.

School reopened at the old Santo Tomas compound in Intramuros; Letran was occupied by the Japanese and the University of Santo Tomas main campus in España was made into an internment camp for Americans. Now, in school, I expounded on sex with authority. And why not? The boys crowded around me as I talked about encounters, the surrender of women and their wantonness when aroused. Much of it was fiction, but not the descriptions of the act; they were realities that I enjoyed almost every night now, or even in the daytime when Corito felt the urge.

3

The war years! How truly memorable they were, not because we suffered—we never did—but because through all those years, my sexual awakening opened up to me a sensual world I would always covet. What are social taboos? They are the absurd and even grotesque creations of society. Look at the Bible—you have everything there: incest, adultery, murder. Does the Bible lose its value because of these depictions? I am not rationalizing my relations with Corito—God knows I love her in the fullest, sincerest measure of the word. Sin is a social definition, not a moral one.

We had a dozen maids, maybe more, of varying ages, from the new addition from the hacienda, this girl Severina, who was sixteen at the time that I was fourteen and a sophomore in high school, to the cook, who was fifty. Severina was very dark when she arrived; I noticed her at once when she served us breakfast for the first time, her slimness, her very good teeth and those big, beautiful eyes. The work in the fields had not only darkened her skin, it had also roughened her hands. But her skin was unblemished and, as I later saw, her thighs were much fairer than her legs.

Severina helped in the kitchen, which meant she had to do the dishwashing, cleaning up and assist in the marketing. Mother actually went to the Quiapo market almost every day in the early days of the war but stopped altogether when transport became difficult, as there was no more gasoline for the cars. We had this *dokar,* actually a glorified calesa with car tires for wheels and drawn by a pony retired from the Sta. Ana racetrack. I often sat beside Severina in the rear, the cook on the other side, when they went to market. I would drop them off in Quiapo first, then proceed to Intramuros. I'd crowd Severina, sit so close to her so that at times my arm would press against her breast. She did not move away.

As the war lengthened, classes became desultory, and I often went home early. I would tarry in the kitchen and talk with Severina as she went about her chores. The cook must have noted my interest but she did not show it. It was only much later that I learned Severina was her niece.

I always felt that I could do anything I pleased with the help. I had seen Mother slap them when they displeased her, and they would whimper, "No, Señora. Yes, Señora." I had also seen Father kick the tenants in the hacienda and whip them with his riding stick, which he always carried even when he was not riding. So I knew I could also do whatever I wished with Severina.

Although this was how I looked at the help, at that age I nonetheless felt some twinge of conscience perhaps, some uneasy feeling, an awkwardness in the mind, but I couldn't stop, a compulsion beyond my control dictated my acts.

The first time I called Severina away from her chores, I said any other maid could do what she was doing, I needed her in my room. It was one of those evenings when I was alone in the house. Corito had gone to visit a friend in Malate, and my parents were off at some official function; my father then was a member of the cabinet. Severina was in her white uniform. Although she was older, I was much taller and heavier. I had a tendency toward obesity like my father and mother, but in later years, I took care of that with a regimen of exercise and diet.

I called Severina from the stairs, and as all the help had been instructed, she came immediately. She was in her bare feet; in the house, the servants were not allowed to wear shoes or slippers so that the floor would always be shiny and clean. It was only we who wore shoes.

The moment she got to my room I told her to lock the door. I suppose that, at that instant, she suspected something untoward would happen, for immediately anxiety clouded her face. But lock the door she did, and then she stood there, waiting. I merely looked at her. The chandelier in the ceiling, the reading lamp on my table were switched on. In that brightness, she truly looked pretty, prim even, in her white uniform.

"Take off your clothes, Severina," I snarled.

She blanched. "No, Señorito," she said.

I was seated on my bed. I stood up and went to her, trying to manage an angry visage, although, to put it frankly, I was quite nervous. "Take them off or I will beat you."

She gaped and for a while I thought she would scream, but she didn't. Then, slowly, she took off her white uniform and, underneath, a white chemise. In those days, girls rarely wore bras. Corito did not, neither did Mother.

Her body, from the breasts down to her thighs, was much fairer than her arms, legs and face, which were exposed to the sun. Her breasts were not large like Corito's. She stood silently, eyes downcast. She cringed as I approached and tilted her chin so she would look at me. Her eyes were misty.

She wore a necklace—a thin strip of leather from which hung what seemed to be a locket but on closer scrutiny turned

out to be a triangular seashell, whitish and smooth, with in-
scriptions that were not legible.

"It is a charm," she explained shyly as I started fingering it.
"It was given to me by my mother when I was small . . . to protect me from harm, or evil. . . ."

"Like me?" I inquired. She did not reply; on her face was this
smile, half free.

"No, Señorito," she whimpered. I fingered her panty.

"Take it off," I growled, raising my hand as if to strike her.
Slowly, she slid it down her legs.

I walked around her slowly, admiring her, comparing her
with Corito's voluptuousness, how slim she was and how little
pubic hair she had compared to Corito. After a while, I told her
to put her dress on, and this she did hastily. I told her to return
to her chores but to slip into my room when everyone in the
maids' quarters was asleep.

※

At this juncture, may I relate again my grandfather's sterling
legacy to this nation. Some are saying now that he was an op-
erator, that he brokered the Biaknabato agreement between
the revolutionaries and the Spanish rulers wherein a lot of
money changed hands. The Cobello name is most honorable
and I will not permit anyone to tarnish it. Whatever my grandfather did was for a larger cause; why should he be blamed if,
in the process, he also profited? Remember that he did not act
on his own, that everything he did was approved by a consen-
sus, by the leaders of the revolution itself. This is not clearly
mentioned in the history books. From what I remember of the
old man, he was at heart a democrat, not an autocrat like my
father or, if you will, like myself.

He had prescience—his eyes focused on the future while his
feet were firmly planted on the ground. He never foreswore his
Spanishness, but he quickly learned the language of the Amer-

icans, much of it self-taught, and thereby placed himself on a plateau far above the other *ilustrados* who didn't know English and couldn't talk with the new hierarchs. The acquisition of a new language is the acquisition of the power to communicate—so inordinately basic—and those who had limited themselves to Spanish found themselves isolated, frustrated, when the Spaniards left. As writers, Rizal and Mabini saw early enough the creeping dominance of English, which was to continue far into the future, and all those noisy Tagalistas, if they believe their nationalist cant, are doomed to be left by the roadside.

Grandfather worked for peace always, be it with the Spaniards or with the Americans who succeeded them. In this regard, my father was merely a continuum of this tradition when, during the occupation by the Japanese, he accepted—maybe sought is a more apt word—a cabinet position in the puppet government.

In the library are pictures of my grandfather, dapper in his gray suit, felt hat and mustache. He is pictured with some of the leaders of the revolution, then with the American governors-general. He was, after all, one of the founders of the Federalista Party, which sought federation with the United States. Later on, with other mestizos, he went to Washington with the first Philippine mission. Father's pictures with Japanese officers and with Prime Minister Tojo when he visited Manila are not on display; they are in a special album and will certainly be displayed when, once more, history shall have made the judgment that collaboration with the Japanese was most honorable. Indeed, time has that ultimate capacity to render the passions of the past when recalled in the present as no more than grandiloquent gestures.

Like I said, I can easily trace my ancestry to Castille in the late eighteenth century; certainly, there was some dilution with a bit of Indio and Chinese blood into our line. But I am arrogantly certain about my illustrious ancestry. Recently, I was so incensed by an article written by this young punk of a historian Lamberto Campo. In it, he implied that my grandfather was a scoundrel, that his wealth was actually embezzled from revolutionary funds entrusted to him. I say, *Qué barbaridad!*

At first, I had thought of filing a libel charge against him, but then I realized it would only polish his ego. I decided, instead, to just let it pass—people forget. If there is anything Filipinos do not have, it is memory. I had thought, of course, of applying the ultimate critique. I could have easily done it and, indeed, it would have been more satisfying and conclusive. I would have had my hirelings do the job, of course—they are always very efficient at whatever chore I give them. But he was not worth all the messiness that could, in the future, bother my conscience.

I have digressed.

Severina feared me at first, but, soon enough, that fear was banished and, afterward, I no longer had to remind her about her nocturnal duties. She seemed to have accepted them as part of her lot. Soon my demands took her out of the kitchen even in the mornings or afternoons. I did not bother to think what the cook thought about it.

We would talk softly far into the night, savoring each other's warmth, and this is how I came to know that she was born in this small island in the Visayas and had lived there until her parents uprooted the family for an equally harsh life in a hacienda—ours. She spoke of white beaches and limestone caves, and spirits that roamed the ether, some of them malevolent. And while she spoke she would clasp the charm hanging from her neck.

I had really grown up. My juvenile fear of lightning and thunder was gone, maybe because during the Occupation, with the Japanese soldiers occupying the schoolhouse below the hill, every so often I heard the sound of their guns when they were drilling. It was on one such stormy night in July that Corito, perhaps missing me, perhaps wondering why I no longer sought her, barged into my room. I had been careless. Or perhaps Severina had forgotten—the latch to the door had not been fastened. Corito stood there watching, Severina suddenly stiff like a block of wood, but how could I stop? How could I? It was as if I didn't hear her at all when she said aloud, "*Puñeta!* You are doing it to a *muchacha!* Have you no *delicadeza* at all?" She stomped off and banged the door just as I was shattered into a million pieces of sheer bliss.

Perhaps, in a very profound manner I did not understand at the time, Severina was my first love. I was not the first, however, and though in my adolescence I couldn't tell, I felt some regret, jealousy even, for the man who had deflowered her. How many chances really can a man get to have that experience with a virgin, particularly these days?

She told me a common enough story about how peasant women were preyed on by the landlords of the time. She was thirteen—she had not gone beyond grade four in the village school, her parents did not have the money for her to go to town five kilometers away to attend the intermediate grades.

"But, you know," she said, pride shining in her eyes, "I can read and write in English better than someone in the village who finished grade seven. . . ." Indeed, I was to learn later how bright she was, how easily she learned Spanish not just from the cook but, I suppose, some of it from me, for soon enough it was in Spanish that I spoke to her, my Tagalog being extremely poor.

"Give me anything to read," she challenged me, and rising naked from my bed, she went to my study table and took the first book there within reach, Philippine history for high schools, and proceeded to read with clear diction the chapter on the discovery of the Philippines. I was simply amazed—it was as if she had been speaking English for a long time.

Let me digress again and explain how Father and his father before him managed Hacienda Esperanza and other properties in Manila. They never really had direct contact with the tenants. The management, the division of the harvest, the collection of rents were all left to caretakers, *encargados.* Depending on their skills and trustworthiness, these men—with education and often small landowners themselves—managed tracts of land and the sugar mill, kept the books, doled out loans, collected our share of the harvest and stayed in the town or the larger villages in the hacienda.

We had a big house at the other end of San Quentin, but we didn't stay there too long, for my parents missed the company of their mestizo friends and those dinners at the Club and the Casino and, most of all, those parties at Malacañang Palace, to which my parents were frequently invited. We did go to San Quentin during the school vacation, sometimes at Christmas—how Father loved playing Santa Claus without the outlandish costume!

On Christmas day, the tenants' children—hundreds of them—gathered in the yard before the house. From the balcony, Father would toss to them fistfuls of new coins. A mad scramble and he would stand there, a supreme look of satisfaction on his face. It was fun for the children, and I would have joined them if Father had not restrained me.

Severina's father had borrowed from the *encargado;* his debts had piled up because of the high interest. There was no way he could really get out of that bog. The *encargado* saw the young girl—"Let her serve in my house in payment of some of your debts," he said. Severina's family knew the implication of that order, but what could they do? The *encargado* could drive them away from the land with the flimsiest excuse, and though they could appeal to my father, seldom did a farmer take this recourse.

This is Severina's story, which she, at first, hesitated to tell:

"I was very young, fourteen, but at that age there are many things that we in the village already know. The work was not difficult—I helped in the kitchen, I scrubbed the floor and went on errands for the mistress, for their children. I rarely saw the *encargado*—he was away most of the time, attending to his land and to the hacienda. But every time he was home, when he was eating with his family and I was serving, always his eyes were on me. And, once, he found me alone in their bedroom scrubbing the floor and, without warning, he started squeezing my breasts till they hurt. I told him, so he stopped.

"Then, one weekend, his family—all of them—went to the city to vacation for two weeks. It was April and warm, and the rains had not yet come. He told me to go to our village with half a sack of rice, which I carried on my head; it was for my family, he said they needed it and, of course, I was grateful for anything that I could bring home.

"I returned late in the afternoon, very tired, because our village was very far from the house. He told me to take a rest, and after supper that night he told me to take a bath, then to go to his room.

"I knew it would happen one day, but I did not expect it so soon, and I really prayed that it wouldn't hurt. I had started menstruating four months before."

Like an eager voyeur, I had asked her to describe her initiation, but although it happened not too long ago, recollecting the details was difficult. What she remembered most was her fear.

I did not realize then the cruelty of what I was doing, and I asked if she had enjoyed it like she was now enjoying our relationship. An immediate and violent shaking of the head. "It was so painful I cried. I thought it would last forever."

She hated the man's breath—it was foul—and his saliva was all over her face. The realization that she was no longer a virgin grieved her more than anything; there was a boy she had grown up with, and she had promised herself she would give that gift to him.

Early on, when I was still in grade school, my father had told me to select my friends not because they possessed good character but because they were rich like us, so that there would be no difference in social status. And knowing them would give some assurance of mutual help in the future. As for women, I should never marry below my class and should look at marriage as a social and economic arrangement. "You cannot let our wealth be broken up, be divided among these villagers." Thus he described the nonmestizos. "Better if you go to Europe and Spain and marry there rather than have your bloodline sullied by them."

I knew then that Severina was just a plaything. I think she knew this, too. It was not easy for me to absorb this view, to get it entwined with my mind and heart, to live with it, and it was just as well, perhaps, that I had to experience this dilemma, this hurt and wrenching away from someone who, I later realized, I had cared for. Not that I became callous, but always I had to think of my position, which should not be eroded by adolescent sentimentalism.

How I missed her! Her aunt, the cook, said simply that she had gone back to Nueva Ecija, but when I inquired from the other help, they said they didn't know for sure that she had returned to the hacienda. I learned much, much later that the cook knew Severina had to leave. Could it be Corito's doing? But Corito said flatly she did not send her away. It was beneath her, she said with imperious disdain, to be jealous of a *muchacha*.

If she went back to the hacienda, for sure the *encargado* would take her again. It would seem that the cook knew this would happen. In afterthought, I did recall Severina saying that she would leave for some distant place in the Visayans, where relatives had migrated earlier. I had completely ignored her, thinking this was a ruse. I had also thought that she was just a body to be possessed, all that brown softness, those shy kisses and the caress that seldom came—all these were embossed in memory, and they would all return as reverie, as remembered bliss so intense as to be almost physical.

My last night with Severina will always be enshrined in my mind and heart. It is all revealed wisdom now why she had acted the way she did—so vivacious, so happy. She did not want our last moments marred by recriminations, by gloom. I did not know it was to be our last so I lived the moment, too. Before she left me, however, I had a last look at the charm. Maybe it was a trick of light, the sallow shadow of the bedpost, a dulled reflection, but the triangle was no longer so white—it seemed streaked with tiny blobs of amber. It had changed color.

4

Severina's absence was somehow soothed by Corito, my dear sister, who was always there, ready and even hungry for my embrace. I do not know if my parents ever suspected my relations with Severina. As for Corito, they were pleased by our seeming closeness, as it augured well for our harmony after they had gone.

Soon, Severina's absence was no longer a nagging ache. As for the war, my parents had talked about its coming. More than once, General MacArthur had come to the house for those splendid parties my parents gave. Once, the general had danced with Corito, which made her so happy she talked about it for days. Major Dwight Eisenhower, who was then MacArthur's aide, came too. He played excellent bridge and was popular with the ladies. When MacArthur sent Eisenhower back to the States, Father said it was because he was jealous.

On the advice of the general and other high officials, Father had ordered the building of an air-raid shelter right in the house, by the porch, a cavern of cement with lights, flush toilet and bunks for six—although there were just four of us. Here, too, was stocked all sorts of supplies, canned food, sacks of rice, beans and even toilet paper. We were never short of food during the war, and we did not touch this reserve until the last year of the war, when there was a shortage of food everywhere. To augment our food supply, a portion of the garden was also planted to vegetables, camote—sweet potato— and cassava; with high walls surrounding it, our house was a fortress against hunger and also the marauding world.

As for the guerrillas, like most Filipino leaders, Father knew how to take care of his flanks and his rear. It was, of course, somewhat of a surprise for me to learn after the war that he was a guerrilla leader—the main reason why he was not imprisoned like Recto and the others who collaborated with the Japanese. I am sure that his friendship with General MacArthur assured him immunity.

My father also did something during the war that only a few people knew about. One of his Japanese friends was General Kuroda, who was fond of the pleasures of the bedroom. Father procured for him from among the impoverished mestizo families in Ermita and Malate who had no way of making a living as the businesses they were all engaged in were closed down.

This was one lesson that the war taught me—that every event in time presents opportunities that are recognizable only to those with enough sensibility to see them, that it is possible to thrive in adversity if the needs of the rulers are pandered to.

But this is going ahead of the story. The war was also for me a time for growing up, for learning how men can rise above the misfortune of others. Big thoughts now in retrospect but, at the time, I was really concerned with just the gonads. With Severina gone and Corito having become a comfortable habit, I wanted something less trite, different.

I am sure Father was only too aware of my physical needs. It was so many years later that I realized he knew of my relations with Severina. One afternoon, he took me to this house in Pasay, which turned out to be ours, although I did not know it until after the war when I had to make an inventory of our real estate properties.

Mid-1944, the Occupation was now on its third year, the Japanese were hated and feared. Guerrillas roamed the countryside and the city itself. Japanese soldiers were often ambushed right in the city, and they took hostages whom they executed at will. Even for us, who were used to so much comfort, there were now inconveniences. Gasoline was rationed and only one of the cars in the garage was running, and was used only when Father and Mother had some special occasion to attend. Most of the time, we used the *dokar*. As I said, life in the city had worsened and many residents had gone to the provinces where some food was available.

The house in Pasay was substantial and was rented by an American businessman who was interned in Santo Tomas. It had a wide yard like the house in Sta. Mesa, with acacia trees. The eight bedrooms were on the second floor. The living room was large. Unlike some of the houses in Pasay, it had a cement wall ten feet high. Such a wall would prove no protection later on, during the battle for Manila. I can only imagine the ferocity of that battle, which engulfed the city south of the Pasig, including Pasay.

I was truly bored. I soon developed some desire for reading. Though the library at home was big and growing bigger with the Filipino first editions that my father bought, both my parents never really read; they were collectors, visiting the Philippine Education Company on the Escolta every so often to see what books were worth adding to the library, what old books on the Philippines were available.

I have digressed again, so let me go back to the house in Pasay and how Father sent me there one afternoon in January.

He had simply instructed me to watch over the place; I suppose that all he wanted really was for my presence to be noted there as some form of deterrent against anything that might be detrimental to him, particularly at this time when the war was turning badly for the Japanese—that, too, was what he said.

I was surprised the moment I entered the house. But first, may I relate the elaborate security at the gate, all of it iron as high as the wall, with a peephole for the guard to ascertain visitors. The opened gate revealed another enclosure within with grills, and before it was opened, two men looked at us and greeted Father very politely. Father had not really told me what it was that I would oversee, but there in the living room, sprawled in various forms of undress, gossiping and eating green mangoes, were a dozen mestizas. I realized soon enough that the house was a brothel, but at the time I did not consider Father's operating it as something socially abominable. In afterthought, what he had done was not unique. As any historian who has studied the Visayan elite will confirm, the Danteses operated not just gambling dens but whorehouses wherefrom they branched into more socially acceptable businesses.

A very corpulent mestiza in her early fifties met us at the door. As if she had known me for years, she greeted me gustily and with a hug. She was all blubber and her perfume was overwhelming. Her greeting in Spanish was very informal, but not the manner with which she addressed Father. Soon, they were in a hush-hush discussion, the same way Father had discussions with Mother when they did not want Corito and me to hear. While they were talking, the girls kept quiet and assumed stiff, formal manners so unlike their comfortable slouch when we had arrived.

Her instructions finished, Señora Meding, as she was called, waddled up to me and embraced me again, her bad breath assailing me. At fifteen, I was big, but she was bigger. No, huge would be the more apt description. She must have weighed at least two hundred and fifty pounds, this at a time when almost every Filipino was losing weight on a diet of gruel and camote tops. I soon learned that the Japanese officers brought not just money but food, and those rice crackers that I liked.

My instructions were simple. I was to stay in the house, keep my eyes and ears alert, and report on the Japanese officers who came at any time of day.

Señora Meding's instructions were different. "I am to see to it that you are not bored and that you stay out of trouble." She took me to the second floor, to Father's room, which was now going to be mine. It overlooked the middle-class houses beyond the high serrated walls, a few vacant lots planted to vegetables as every empty lot in Manila then was planted to camote or talinum.

Then, before she turned to go, Señora Meding did something that shocked me. She fondled my crotch and smiled. "There are a dozen of them here. I do not see how this"—she pressed it firmly, pleasurably—"can be idle."

Father's bedroom was larger than the other rooms and had shelves filled with the books—novels mostly, some poetry, history—the American tenant had left. In a sense, it was in that room that I first learned to appreciate literature, having so much leisure to make use of. After a time, let me say this, if sex is freely available, it can become a terrible bore.

For many of us, whatever our social background, war was an experience that tested character, enabling people to recognize not so much their strengths but their weaknesses. I knew then that I was a sensualist, that I craved whatever pleased the senses, be it a gourmet dish or a woman in all her glory, the fine down on the back of her neck, the narrow waist broadening into her buttocks, those limbs down to the dainty feet and, of course, I must not forget the beautiful mounds of her breasts. As for food, there were the delicacies that the Japanese officers brought, dried fish and various kinds of pickles and pastes, all of which I learned to appreciate.

A dozen mestizas who were anxious to be in the embrace of a young lion entertained Japanese officers only, and they told me they smelled of fish and soy sauce and performed mechanically. Was this automatic performance attributable to their culture, which regarded women as inferior? As my reading of Japanese history later showed, there was a time when the Japanese killed baby girls at birth.

I had planned on going home every evening, but soon enough decided to stay in Pasay for days at a time. The brothel's varied delights enthralled me. I would like to describe these sensual intimacies in some detail, but I have never really appreciated pornography.

Not one of the girls was over twenty. I cannot now remember them all, but one left me not just with a memory but something physical that the reader will soon know about.

Adela reminded me of Severina. She was mestiza but was what we call *morena,* brown with classic features. Afterward, when I started taking pictures, I realized that she had photogenic features and her face could have easily propelled her to stardom, our movies being what they are, nothing but vehicles for lousy actors and actresses with mestizo features. Adela's skin was pure—not one blemish on her entire body. Her thighs were a lighter shade, as were her belly and her breasts. She would stand before me, pleased by my admiration of her body, and I would simply watch her and be mesmerized by that animal splendor. In the heat before the advent of the cool months, she moved about my room in her pristine beauty. I wonder if the Japanese officers appreciated her as much as I did, having seen afterward the ivory luster of the skin of Japanese women.

During my stay in Pasay, I became friendly with Colonel Masuda, who was in charge of the propaganda corps. It must always be remembered that my father's brothel was exclusively for high-ranking officers—no lower than a colonel. He was a graduate of one of the California universities and his English was much better than mine. We had the same weakness—we both wanted Adela. He came once a week, and if Adela was in my room, I had to let her go. I was jealous; I asked her what kind of a man he was. Like my sister, Adela had gone to an exclusive girls' college in Ermita, but when the war came, her father lost his business. Unlike us, the family had no other resources. They had no land in the province, and there was no rent to collect on their real estate in Manila. Now, she was feeding a family of six living in a lovely Ermita home, but without the affluence to maintain their old lifestyle.

Looking back, I realize how tenaciously some images of adolescence linger, how the adult mind feeds on this remembered past. Its hurts are magnified and the transient pleasures even more so, so that in recollection, all these seem to have occurred only recently. In those moments with Adela, I never fully accepted her as a whore.

She told me the Japanese were losing, that the Americans were already in Leyte, this at a time when the *Tribune* flatly stated they were still in the South Pacific, island-hopping, that it would take them a hundred years to reach the Philippines in that slow process. It was now late in 1944, and fewer and fewer officers were coming to the brothel. Manila was bombed in September of that year by American carrier planes, dark like drones in the sky, more than a hundred of them, the hum of their engines cascading down into the starving city. I was in my room with Adela. I remember this moment in history very well; I was at the height of my physical exertions and couldn't stop. Adela had become tense but I had to fulfill destiny, and only when it was over did we go out, not knowing then how dangerous it was, as falling shrapnel from Japanese antiaircraft shells had killed several Filipinos.

Colonel Masuda came early that evening. I remember bits of our conversation, how he missed his country, his wife and child, how he hoped someday all this nastiness would be over and we would meet again.

I appreciated his candor, his offer of friendship, young as I was. He was different from the other officers. I think he knew from the very beginning that Japan couldn't win, which gave his conversation at times a tone of melancholy and, at other times, an arrogance that was so unlike him.

We were both in the living room and he had brought along some sake and those rice crackers. Someone had beaten him to Adela and he was going to wait. He was not interested in any other girl.

"Young man." He always called me thus. I did not resent his patronizing attitude. "We are a great nation. Look at the map, and realize that my country is small, that it is mountainous and many of my countrymen are still poor. We Japanese are destined to lead. We Japanese . . ." He did not continue as his eyes traveled to the ceiling, the plaster already cracked, and then he sighed.

It was one of those seemingly quiet October evenings—the tremor of war muted, distant. Manila no longer had electricity, but we had candles. Many residents had already sought refuge in the provinces; the air raids had become incessant and the Japanese no longer fired their antiaircraft guns; they let the American pilots fly at will over the city. We were not to leave Manila, however. We had enough food stashed in the air-raid shelter and were safer in the city, too, although, at the time, I did not think any place was safe at all.

Colonel Masuda's last visit to Pasay gladdened me, for now I was assured Adela would have more time for me. He stood up after a while, removed his sword and his khaki jacket. He had also shucked his boots, which, for the first time, I noticed were not polished. In his white shirt, without the full trappings of his uniform, his head clean-shaven as always, he did not look forbidding at all; there was something boyish about him. It was not the sake that had made him more relaxed, I think; it was the fact that he could speak in English to a sixteen-year-old. What he said did not fully register then, but it did with Father when, as usual, I recounted it to him.

There was not a single sign that he was drunk; as always, his English was lucid. "From the very beginning," he admitted finally, "I knew we would lose this war. I have lived in America and I know how vast, how powerful that country is, particularly when it is aroused. And we Japanese have never been able to think logically, rationally, because we are too sentimental, because we are overcome too easily by emotion, by mass hysteria. You do not know what that means—you Filipinos, you do not have a nation." He then proceeded to explain Pearl Harbor—an explanation that was wasted on me for I did not know Japan then as well as I do now—now that I am in partnership with them.

"I agree with General Kuroda. Do you remember him?"

I nodded. Only later did I learn that the general was commander in chief of the Japanese army in the country.

"General Kuroda was correct. He said this country cannot be defended—so he spent his time playing golf and chasing women. . . . I leave for Leyte tomorrow," he continued. "And there I will die." He then told me that the Americans had returned in full force, that in a matter of weeks they would be in Manila and in a few months in Tokyo. He smiled and poured the sake into the glass. "If I live through this, and I doubt very much I will, remember that I said the Americans are benevolent victors. My country won't suffer very much."

His talk meandered, then he paused and confronted me: "So you love Adela—you are much too young to know what true love is. What do the Americans call it? Puppy love?" He snickered.

I was extremely embarrassed. Who could have told him? Could Señora Meding have told him? But the madam seldom talked with the officers; she always stayed in the background, letting the girls do that themselves. Adela, then, must have told him and, for an instant, I loathed her for making my innermost feelings a subject of gossip. She must have cared for this officer old enough to be her father, this bald, smelly, bowlegged man with buck teeth. Why do women tell other women (or men) of their conquests? Does doing this make them proud, more sure of their capacity to ensnare?

I learned from this vivid chapter of my youth that you never, never make women too sure of your feelings, least of all express them in an endearment. Possess them, pamper them if you must, but never, never utter the word. For one, they will try to squeeze it out of you with their wiles, which are most enjoyable. Keep them wondering where their physical and other forms of affectionate expression have failed.

Colonel Masuda drank his sake. He offered me a glass. I did not want to disappoint him, particularly after he had said, "I was keeping this bottle for some happy event, but there is going to be no happy event." He raised his glass in a toast and then thrust it so roughly against my glass I almost dropped it. "To the past and, most of all, to tonight."

Adela was finished with her customer, an officer I had not seen before. She accompanied him to the door, a dour-looking man who, in his uniform, looked more like a hotel doorman. Now free, she went to Colonel Masuda, whose countenance had changed; he seemed more gregarious. Adela sat beside the colonel on the sofa and put her arm around his shoulders.

"Do you know?" he continued talking to me, "in spite of our great military power, we are a poor people. Our farmers sell their daughters to prostitution as a matter of habit, and thousands of our women . . . we send them all over Asia not just to comfort our soldiers but to earn money for Japan."

I remembered Severina and wondered to what dismal and obscure corner of the country she had been flung, if she was in Nueva Ecija at all. A sharp stab in the heart, but it passed quickly and I continued listening to this officer holding Adela's hand.

"I have a young daughter like her." He turned briefly to Adela. "Thank heavens she is a girl, or she would have been conscripted into the army. College students, they are sending them to the front. Farm boys—that is what most of our soldiers are. And I, a college professor, what am I doing in this uniform?" He paused, then laughed, but his laughter was without mirth.

"It is all a game, a terrible game," he said after a while. "The leaders, the statesmen, the generals who play it . . ." Then he jabbed a finger at me. "You are all playing games. Your father, I know, he is playing a game, too."

I tensed immediately. This is what Father had asked me to be attentive to, what these officers said that pertained to him, to their plans, to our safety and future. Young as I was, I already knew how dangerous the times were, that we must use our wits to survive.

"Your father," he said with a sneer, "will come out a winner because he senses opportunity. He dances to our tune but he would sooner stop that and dance to the American tune even before they arrive. That is how colonial elites not only survive but flourish." He laughed derisively. Afterward, when the horrors of that war had ended, I realized how perceptive Colonel Masuda was.

Then he did something that I will never forget. He started taking off his uniform till he was almost naked but for that strip of white cloth like a G-string over his loins.

"I will teach you jujitsu," he announced. He was really drunk and one does not argue with drunks. "Take off your clothes," he commanded in that guttural manner of the Japanese. I have heard of jujitsu but had never seen it as practiced by the people who invented it. Like him, I stripped to my shorts. In the meantime, he had pushed the coffee table and the rest of the furniture against the wall so that there was ample space for us in the middle of the living room.

At sixteen, with my mestizo genes, I was taller and heavier than he. "The principle," he said, "is for a smaller person to use the strength of a bigger person to defeat him." He led me to the center of the living room. By now, the cook, Señora Meding and a couple of the maids had come out to watch; except for Adela, all the other girls were busy in their rooms.

"Imagine you have a knife," he said. "Come charging at me."

I thought I would simply humor him. But then, recognizing how short he was, I thought I could knock him over. It was also an opportunity for me to express my displeasure and, I suppose, much of my jealousy. I charged. I was surprised to feel myself flung in the air like a feather. I fell on my back, more embarrassed than hurt. He stood over me, grinning in triumph.

He drew me to my feet, the alcohol in his breath and that peculiar odor of the Japanese assailing me. "This is how you do it," he said. He took my hand and had me poised, then in slow motion, explained how jujitsu worked. It all looked so simple and, indeed, it was when it was my turn to use his strength against him.

We did not put our clothes back on. In our semi-nakedness, we went back to our sake. The bottle was almost empty. He told me to pour all of it into his glass, which I did. He sighed, "But war is not jujitsu. It is not personal combat. The principle does not apply to machines. In war, what is important is who has more. Oil. Resources." He was now speaking in a monologue. "They knew all this in Tokyo—those military men are not stupid. But the emotions ruled, the mood was for war. And if there were people who did not want it, they kept their mouths shut, like I did. That is how it is in Japan. You speak out your mind and you are shunned. The nail that sticks out is hammered down—a common Japanese proverb."

He sat there, shaking his head, then he took Adela by the hand and together they went up to her room, the colonel swaying so on the staircase I thought he would fall. One of the maids picked up his clothes and his sword and followed them up the steps.

He stayed the whole night and was awakened in the morning by aides. Adela and I saw him off—how he had changed in the hollow of one night! Now he was stern of visage, no longer the vulnerable officer made voluble by sake. He hugged Adela, shaking his head, mumbling, "I am very sorry for you. You should not have done it."

We shook hands firmly. He said, "Be very careful when you shake hands with the Japanese—you might be giving them a chance to throw you down. Take care of her," he said stiffly, turning to Adela, who had begun to cry. The aides walked him to the car that would take him back to his unit, and to the fate that implacably awaited him.

5

With Colonel Masuda gone, I should have been pleased. Now there was no visitor to the casa who always sought Adela. The rest who came were not choosy; whoever was free was acceptable. The girls, after all, were all young and firm.

Almost immediately after the colonel left, I went to Sta. Mesa to report to Father my strange encounter. He was in the library, surrounded by all those books he would never read. I should remind the reader that it was during the war when there were no classes that I really learned to read, first the novels that opened new vistas to me, then later on the books on history, anthropology and so on. It was about ten in the morning and cool. Overhead, another flight of American planes roared over the roofs, their noise drowning out all sounds, then explosions reverberating from the west as they bombed the few remaining ships in the bay.

Father was reading the *Tribune,* which still came out proclaiming on the front page that the Americans were being pushed to the sea in the south.

"Colonel Masuda has left for Leyte," I told him.

He put the paper down. Father liked the colonel, maybe because he spoke English. Father often talked with him. "So they are going to put up a stand in Leyte then," he said, appearing thoughtful.

"He also said you are playing a double game, Father."

Father bolted upright, his face suddenly ashen. He stared blankly into the sun-flooded patio, then, after a while, his head drooped as if some tragic news had been relayed to him. He had not lost weight as had so many in Manila. With all our private resources, I am sure even our dogs were eating better than most people.

"Adela is the girl that Colonel Masuda often takes?" he suddenly asked.

"Yes, Father," I said.

Somehow a grin came across his face. "That *morena*. At least that Japanese has good taste. And Adela is very good. . . ."

I had always taken for granted that my father tested all the merchandise before they were displayed.

"Go back to Pasay," he said. "Ask Adela if Colonel Masuda told her anything about me."

I would have gone immediately but Corito had seen me; she had followed me to the library and waited for my conversation with Father to end. I turned to leave, but she grabbed my arm. She was displeased—no, she was angry. Why have I kept away? There was no denying her and, meekly, I followed her to her room. While her torrent of reproach gushed forth, she tore off my clothes.

Corito released me at noon from her almost insatiable clutch.

By this time, as I said, fewer officers came—it seemed they were always moving. Whereas there was once some laughter among them, now, except when they had had something to drink, gloom seemed to pervade even their relationships with the girls.

It was late afternoon, the girls were chatting, playing cards, waiting for *merienda* in the living room. I headed for my room and gestured to Adela to follow. She took her time and, by the time she arrived, I had already stripped to my shorts. She fell on me in the manner of welcome I always appreciated.

At sixteen, a man's energies are easily recharged and rekindled and I look back to those days of rapid recovery with nostalgia and longing.

"Your boyfriend may not come back," I said.

She pinched me. "You are jealous, aren't you?"

I nodded.

She hugged me tighter. "But I won't miss him," she said. "He never gave me pleasure like you do."

She had never discussed with me the men she entertained, part of her discreet nature, I suppose, but this time I asked her what she meant. What she told me was amazing. It was my first awareness of Japanese kinkiness, something that was confirmed again and again in their fiction, their motion pictures.

Adela always seemed comfortable when she was like this, moving about in my room. I wanted her like this. She slid down from over me to my side and continued her incredible story.

"All the time we were together, he never did it!" Wistfulness, like some regret, rimmed her voice. "Always he asked me to undress, then he would look at me with such longing—I know—and he would caress me a bit, kiss me very softly, just our lips touching. At first I thought he was impotent, but there was that bulge down there. I would touch it, but he would push me away." Then Adela laughed.

"But last night," she continued with delighted giggles, "when he was there on my bed, drunk and half asleep, and in his G-string, I started playing with it because it was so hard and erect. I mounted him, and he responded, maybe not too consciously. And then he came—exploded inside me—it was not a trickle but a flood. And that was when he became fully conscious, and he stood up and pushed me away roughly. I almost fell off the bed. Then he stood up and started cursing me. Oh, he was really mad. He kept repeating, 'You bitch, now see what you have done. Oh, my God, why did you do it!' As if I had committed a mortal sin. Then, you know something, he held me tenderly and said he was so sorry, and he started to cry. Not loud like a baby, but he was shuddering and tears just came to his eyes. Now, tell me, why should a man do that. I was beginning to wonder, you know, if I wasn't pretty enough for him, or good enough in bed. I suppose I will never know the reason now."

Of course, I didn't know the reason then. Only long afterward did I realize how much Colonel Masuda cared for Adela, how he had vainly tried to protect her from himself.

I asked her if the colonel ever talked about my father. She tried to think back, then she brightened up and said, "Well, this may refer to him. He said that all these wealthy Filipinos working with them—they are all opportunists just waiting for the Americans to come back. Not like those nationalist peasants. . . . What did he mean by that?"

I did not know enough then of the Sakdals and the peasant groups that collaborated with the Japanese out of simple conviction. I did not want to leave yet, but Father had been explicit, I should tell him immediately what Colonel Masuda told Adela.

I slept in Sta. Mesa that night. When Father and I talked, somehow, we always went to the library, as if those books encouraged profundity. Even when I was a child, Father used to lecture to me there to help me grow into maturity. As I grew older, these talks became longer; they were more monologues, for though I was not forbidden to talk back and was encouraged even to argue, I felt inadequate. "You have grown very fast," Father said, noting that I was now taller than he. I often wondered if he and Mother knew or suspected my relationship with Corito. They had remarked quite often on how wonderful it was that, since there were just the two of us, we were very close. I suppose they envisioned no quarrels between us, particularly since we were going to inherit property; when their rich relatives died, the children swooped on their inheritance like vultures, quarreling with one another.

"You must always remember," Father said, "that our wealth must be preserved so that you will both live always in comfort, beholden to no one but yourselves. And you, because you are a man, will be a leader—this is explicit. To lead, you must be strong—and cunning. Know people and how to control them. To see opportunities before others do, then exploit these opportunities. Even war has its opportunities, and those who grab them not only survive but profit. . . ."

It was not easy to understand what Father said then and, certainly, I could not see the opportunities he was talking about. Only when I started out did I, upon looking back, realize that even his brothel eloquently attested to his shrewdness.

Then Father asked, "Who do you think will win this war?"

Without hesitation I replied, "The Americans."

He laughed aloud, then shook his head dolefully. "But it is the Japanese who rule us now, who possess the power over our very lives . . ." He stood up and paced the floor, head bowed, hands behind his back. He was in a white drill suit, as were most of the high officials at the time. He spoke slowly, certainly not to me in particular, shaping his thoughts deliberately. "When this war is over, as with the war with America, many will be accused of collaboration with the enemy—the Japanese. As in the past, too, many will claim patriotism. For others, it will be for sheer survival. But my father, he knew which way the wind would blow. How can the Japanese ever beat the Americans? All they have to do is look at the map! Their defeat of Russia was not overwhelming; Russia was undeveloped. But America is mighty. Still, there will be those naive individuals— pity them—who collaborate with the Japanese sincerely because they believe in them. This old man, Ricarte* . . ."

Father remembered him—irascible, unbending like Mabini. He is irrelevant now and may be forgiven his stubbornness and senility. My father loathed him and so did I.

"When he returned from Japan the other year, he had so much faith in the Japanese. He must be repenting now." He stopped and turned to me. "I cite him so that you will understand when I say that convictions can cripple a man. A conviction that should never be changed is the conviction of self-preservation."

※

I went to Pasay, urged not by the stern demand of duty but by the seductive call of the flesh. Toward December, there were few visitors, but there was enough food stored in the house so that all the girls stayed. Each of them had some loot from her customers stashed in her room. A bottle of sake, some bean cakes, dried fish even. Some had watches—two or three each— which the Japanese officers must have grabbed from helpless victims.

I saw less and less of Father. Mother said he was attending to official business. He had considered taking us to Baguio when the whole hierarchy of government fled there. We had a house there that was well maintained, but Father said Sta. Mesa was far safer than Baguio or Manila.

---

*General Artemio Ricarte refused to pledge allegiance to the United States after the Spanish-American War, went into exile in Japan, and returned to the Philippines with the Japanese army in 1942.

I was in Sta. Mesa when the Americans arrived; Father had sent for me and told me to look after Corito and Mother. I didn't want to, but I was very glad later on that I did return. Throughout that hellish week in February, the sound of battle reached us and, from our vantage point, we could see the city burning, the smoke darkening the sky, the fires lighting up the night. We had a moment of fear one night when the Japanese, perhaps a company or even more, marched by the house, their boots and voices ominous in the dark. But they did not bother us, nor the people down the hill. It was from them that we learned Manila south of Pasig was completely destroyed.

Father was nowhere. Mother assured me he was safe, that he had gone to the north to meet the Americans. I had the *dokar* harnessed and hurried to Pasay, where I learned that the Americans were already in complete control of the city.

Although it happened more than thirty years ago, the scene is still as fresh in my mind as if it was only this morning that I beheld it. Then and only then did I realize the senseless ferocity of war. Everywhere I turned in this city that was once so very familiar to me was nothing now but the rubble and blackened ruins of stone buildings. All the bridges across the Pasig were in shambles, the Escolta was burned, as were portions of Quiapo. The Americans had stretched pontoon bridges on the river and I crossed on foot, as did many weary civilians. Along the way, more ruins, the Post Office, the Metropolitan Theatre where the whole family had listened to concerts conducted by Herbert Zipper, the Legislative Building, the University of the Philippines complex and, to my right, the spires of the Intramuros churches were no more, and those thick and heavy walls were torn with huge gaps. Along the streets, the electric posts, the trees were broken and ravaged by shells; shrapnel lay everywhere and, where the dead were yet uncollected, the overwhelming stench of carrion pervaded the air.

All of the neighborhood in Pasay was cindered ruin. Nothing of our house remained except the blackened walls. Nothing. The trees were shattered, too. There was no one in the vicinity I could talk to, who could tell me if there were survivors, particularly a sweet young prostitute with clear brown skin, a dimpled chin and eyes that sparkled always. I was later told that all the people in the neighborhood had fled to the Rizal Memorial Stadium nearby, and that was where the Japanese had massacred them.

I never saw Adela again, but I will never, never forget her. What she left scarred me. In afterthought, I now realize why Colonel Masuda, the gentleman that he was, did not want to touch her. Before Christmas, she had developed a sore on her lip that wouldn't go away and, very soon after, I developed a sore, too—not big, but it, too, wouldn't disappear till after a time. It was the unmistakable symptom that, at the time, I did not know. Colonel Masuda loved Adela, perhaps much more than I did, but it was from him that she and Corito and I got this dread disease.

Soon enough, the city was normal. Running water and electricity were restored in certain parts, and all sorts of GI goods were on sale on the sidewalks—American cigarettes, K rations. Army trucks became the first buses, plus a few old ones that were rehabilitated. The jeepneys soon appeared. Father was given four jeeps by the government, as our cars, which hadn't run for a year or so, were all rusted. The hacienda, which we had not visited during the war, was overrun by the Huks, but they were soon driven out by the army and the civilian guards. As for Father, again, the truism of what he told me about seeking opportunities was evident.

I was quite surprised that he was honored by the Americans—they even made him a colonel. It turned out that all along he was a guerrilla—the double game that Colonel Masuda had so aptly described. I don't know how he did it, but the citation is there on the wall. Nothing that I saw or heard during the war years indicated his valor, his capacity for conspiracy. But there are really quite a few things I never knew about him, or about my grandfather. Perhaps it is best that I did not bother.

My dear sister got married almost a decade after the war. Manila was no longer rubble; the Manila Hotel, where so many social functions were held, was renovated. Our Sta. Mesa house intact, untouched by vicissitudes, was remodeled and equipped with central air-conditioning. The wide garden that was planted partly to okra, eggplants, tomatoes and pechay had long been replanted with bermuda grass. There was no power in our part of the city after the war, but Father had obtained a generator from the U.S. Army, whose highest officials, including General MacArthur, were his prewar friends. All the past magnificence of the house—Mother's silver and china, which were not looted—were on display again, as if no misery had ever ravaged this city.

The long gowns, the tuxedos, the cultivated flamboyance were, however, no longer in sight. The mestizo elite, sustained by raucous snobbery, was there—by now, I could recognize them, their illustrious names, their bland, smug faces. There was, however, one person who was certainly missed, whose munificent favors had flowed to all of us in that wedding reception. If he were alive, he would have been the godfather; Quezon had died of tuberculosis in the United States. But, from the wisps of conversation that evening, he was present in spirit.

Corito's husband was a tall, handsome mestizo. His forebears, like mine, had also figured in the revolution, and knowing this, I often wonder if there were any Indio leaders in the revolution at all. From the very beginning, when he was courting Corito, I was somehow bothered by this quality of sinuous strangeness about him, an illusive allure that soon clarified itself. I was really growing up, not just intellectually but in perception, this time of sexual perversity. Camilo was taller than me, and he even had a mustache, which he often flattened with his thumb—a mannerism he couldn't get rid of, and he did this often when he was talking. He had long, thin fingers, almost like a woman's, but there was nothing effeminate in his gestures. His eyes seemed very sharp, fidgety, and when he talked to people he didn't look them in the eye. I don't know what Corito saw in him, but then I think my parents and Camilo's parents had something to do with the marriage.

The wedding reception did not last long—not as long as the parties in the house before the war, when some of the guests stayed on for breakfast. Before midnight, all the guests had departed except for the waiters clearing up the mess in the wide grounds. The dining tables had been set under a canopy of white U.S. Army parachutes, for the rainy season had started. Fortunately, it did not rain that night.

I had become drowsy quite early and had gone to my room where I listened desultorily to the music coming from the aging Serafin Payawal and his orchestra on the terrace. I had also drunk a little wine—I suppose there were still a few cases in the air-raid shelter that Father had stocked. I was partial to white and to port. I was soon asleep.

It must have been around two in the morning—the whole house was quiet. In the kitchen there was no more clatter. From the street one heard the occasional jeep, the music of crickets in the trees. I was awakened by something soft, scented and familiar. Corito was fondling me, kissing me, her mouth tasting of wine, too.

And what about Camilo?

In the soft slight light, I could see the disdain on her face. With me in tow, we went to her bedroom—her bed larger now, a matrimonial bed. Our eyes had gotten used to the dark and, sprawled there, asleep and snoring loudly, was her husband, still in the white suit of the groom.

"He did not do it," Corito said, not bothering to lower her voice. I was now sure Camilo's failure was more than drunkenness. He seemed endowed with virility, and with his mustache he oozed machismo. But sprawled there, his mouth agape, he looked slovenly and dissipated.

Corito shook him, but he slept on. At that very moment, the idea suddenly bloomed in my mind, effulgent, seductive. I realized the risk, and perhaps that was precisely what quickened my pulse, inflamed me. Corito did not need any encouragement. Right there, beside her husband in the deep throes of drunken stupor, we did it willfully, savagely and with delicious vengeance. Corito moaned and heaved, her back arched, her embrace maniacal in its intensity, and through all that tumultuous and noisy passion, Camilo snored on.

6

In the muddied depths of my own being, there is one clear thought that glitters through: I want to die. God, how I wish the end would come so that I would finally be free from these villainous realities about which I can do nothing. Let me sink quickly into that black and rimless murk from where there is no returning, in which there is no consciousness, no bliss. Let it be—after all, my passing will be as insignificant as the demise of insects, living things no less with rights to the sunlight, the sweet air. But they can flit about with their wings while I cannot move on my own feet. They can drink the nectar of flowers as pure as the morning has made it—and what is it that I imbibe but the cruel adulterations that my ailing system needs? How many times have I tried to hold my breath but in the end had to gasp and drink deep, large drafts of the conditioned air?

They watch me with leering eyes, immobile and helpless though I am, with those infernal machines nearby, ever ready to pump oxygen into my lungs and blood into my arteries. Just let me die, I plead with them, but they think I am simply joking, and maybe I am, for in spite of these dark and dangerous thoughts, they know that I wake up, expectant, that another day has come, and that, perhaps, this time, there will be some happy change, no matter how subtle, no matter how trite.

Twelve of them in four-hour shifts, so they will always be alert. All registered nurses and physical therapists, delectably pretty. They pamper me with professional ministration and saccharine coquetry—I have promised that a one-year bonus— and they know it could be more than that—would go to anyone who could make me respond as a man again to their touch. God, how I miss it now, more than food, more than anything in the world.

In the morning, they lift me from my bed and lay me carefully in a tub of warm water. I have grown thinner—the hardness in my muscles has long given way to a flabbiness, a looseness of the skin, which has wrinkled and is more pale now than it ever was. I dread looking at that dead instrument that once could be as hard as a truncheon—that now is no more than a dried and wrinkled eggplant.

They take turns washing my loins, hoping they can, by some prayer or miracle, make it spring to life. I wait eagerly, hopefully, prayerfully, for them to succeed. But they never do.

They wipe me dry and spread baby powder all over my body. I know I exude the odor of an old man—sour, repugnant—and who would want to smell me now as I used to smell my Angela when she was a baby! Ah, that heavenly scent of a baby! What vaporizes from my pores are the ignoble odors of the posterior, of the sick, of the dying! They lavish me with care, but not because they have some loyalty to me, as I know a wife would care for an invalid husband, wipe his anus and handle his excreta, taking all these not as sacrifice but as manifestation of love, for this is the least love can do. For none of them love me. I am clearheaded enough to realize this, which I was not when I was virile. Now, it is only my money that they care about, that the world is interested in. So let it be—I will not drown in illusion. I will not wallow in the muck of self-pity. I will enjoy this wealth vicariously if I can. They put me in a smock and, over it, a thin blanket; it could be cold, but it would make no difference, for my extremities are impervious now to temperature. Except for my face.

My breakfast is ready, but it is like baby food, pureed, homogenized, soft-boiled and without salt—the ultimate punishment! I take in everything with a glass straw. I am tempted to bite it, to swallow those shards so that my intestines, my stomach would be lacerated and I would finally die. Ah, to drink Dom Perignon with a straw, steak blended into an abominable liquid. No, no, not those juicy chunks that linger and please the palate.

✠

As I had always suspected, he was homosexual. I recognized Camilo's sexual deviation even before he married my sister. On those occasions that he visited before he and Corito got married, he would greet me with so much brotherly affection, a tight hug, a lingering handshake and the unmistakable look of lust on his face. In a sense, he confirmed my male attractiveness. I wondered what drove him into this marriage. It was only later that I realized it was for convenience. Father was misinformed. Camilo's family, it turned out, was not so secure after all; much of their property was mortgaged as collateral in the many loans that Camilo's father had taken out. Moreover, he had gambled, kept mistresses and by himself managed to waste their wealth so that when he died shortly after Camilo's wedding, their estate was divided among eight children and Camilo's share was not sufficient to enable him to live in comfort. He was going to be dependent on Corito's largesse.

Whatever nastiness there was between Corito and me later

on, there was one quality about her that made me confident she would not squander her share. She was very careful with money, a result I am sure of Mother's constant lecturing; she was not going to let any man, Camilo included, and her lovers in the future, take advantage of her.

Back to school—this time at the Ateneo. Letran's élan had diminished; Ateneo was attracting upper-class Filipinos, most of them future leaders of the nation. It was necessary that I be enrolled there. I never noticed it till someone wrote about it— look at the children in the public schools, how thin, how malnourished they look and, almost always, they had bad teeth and their skins were blemished. But look at all those boys at La Salle and Ateneo, the girls in the elite women's colleges—how well scrubbed, how well fed they all look.

I took for granted such blatant differences, understood them as fate, as an inevitable condition of the world. I was not going to grieve over it, but I was not going to exploit it or condone it either. That would have been callous of me. I retained fond memories of Severina, and it was from such a station that she came. Ah, Severina—she always evoked from me such sweet nostalgia, that tenderly painful remembering of the first love. Perhaps, because I am now in this parlous condition, memory is more poignant.

There is no better preparation for leadership than the study of the law, that's what Father said, although he himself did not study law. He had no need to; he had hired the best lawyers. I doubt very much if they had helped. Most of the justices in the Supreme Court and the Court of Appeals and a host of judges were his personal friends, his having been a cabinet minister in Quezon's government. After the war, he was also elected senator and as such was noted for his urbanity, civic spirit and, before I forget, his sterling nationalism. And because it had become fashionable, he also made some anti-American speeches. This insight that I learned from him served me well, as you can see.

So law it was. In the meantime, because of those idle days during the Occupation, I developed a habit of reading, as I've said, even those upstart novels written by Filipinos. Like my father, I boasted of an interest in things Filipino, antiques, folk crafts and, in the process, became involved with the plight of our ethnic minorities. It is really so easy to beguile the so-called nationalist intelligentsia with professions of passionate involvement with Philippine culture, especially if such a profession is amply illustrated. Such is the case with Father's collection of rare Philippine books, which he never read but collected avidly. It was natural for me to have continued this interest, and there even came a time when I was acknowledged to have some expertise in Philippine bibliography; actually, I had hired a retired librarian to give some order to the books in the house.

I considered it a duty to continue and improve on my father's collection. After the war, I embarked on trips around the country, looking up rotting churches, gathering antiques, abandoned furniture, old paintings, religious images—*santos*—so that in time several rooms of the Sta. Mesa house were simply bursting with the stuff. That august residence soon acquired the stature of a museum to be visited by culture vultures as well as those scholars interested in this nation's cultural artifacts and its pre-Hispanic past.

As for the ethnic minorities, I championed their cause, for which they honored me and made me chieftain, sultan or whatever was the highest title they could give their leaders.

My forays into their isolated areas also enabled me to map out their mineral deposits, timber resources and whatever could be exploited from this nation's natural bounty. And the sensual satisfaction! As chieftain, I had access to the tribal feminine treasure trove—in fact, in most instances, such treasures were offered to me. But let it not be forgotten that I did help them, perhaps wrongly as some anthropologists have criticized—but what have these mealymouthed academics done for them? There was no tribe that was not welcome in Sta. Mesa, and the quarters in the back that were reserved for our tenants and servants was their home whenever they came to Manila.

My travels to these isolated regions sparked my interest in travel in general, and let it not be forgotten that I have also helped the tourism industry. In the late fifties, I set up one of the first travel agencies in the country, about which I will speak more.

Now, there is another mestizo landlord who tried to imitate me. He had conned several professors and American journalists into writing about his tribal "discoveries." The phony! I was told by impeccable sources he even buried shards of old porcelain in caves so his nitwit believers could dig and find them.

Again, a willful digression. I was concerned that my nationalism not appear as a pose the way it was with my father. This country is crawling with poseurs, impostors, charlatans, especially in the press and in so-called intellectual circles. I have nothing but contempt for these people, these writers who canonize themselves with their pious pronouncements but whose lives are without piety, least of all virtue. Beware of Filipinos who make brilliant speeches—underneath that dazzling verbiage is a dubious personality, maybe ruthless and corrupt, for good men never have to say anything—their deeds speak loudest for them.

Deeds indeed! Let it not be said that I have not acted charitably for others. But let me go on with the story—there is always time to indulge in self-glorification but less for self-pity.

I had often been tempted to accede to Camilo's unspoken invitation. Just simple acquiescence when he gave one of those brotherly hugs would have led to something more conclusive. I can never forget his wedding night, when Corito and I celebrated it in his unfeeling presence. What would have happened if he woke up? Would he have made it a ménage à trois as the French call it?

When Corito gave birth to Angela soon after, I am sure Camilo knew the darling baby wasn't his. Did he bother at all? Did he accuse my sister, or needle her about who the father was? Corito said he treated the baby as his own, and whatever his suspicions, he kept his peace. The price of disturbing the harmony in the house was a risk he did not want to take. But this only for the time being.

🕱

I did not finish my law. Father died with his boots on, as we often say. I always knew he had a mistress, not just one, for it turned out there were four. I don't know how he did it but there were no illegitimate children. No one contested his will. In the first place, he took good care of his women, providing them with houses, substantial properties to sustain them. He was a senator then and the salacious fact of his death was known to all his friends, to us in the family certainly, but there was not a single wisp of scandal in the newspapers. Long before he died, he showed me a list of the journalists who regularly got money from him. I was to continue the time-honored practice. So you see what I mean when I say we shouldn't believe all those vaulting *pronunciamientos* of columnists.

"At least," Father said when Angela was born, "I saw my grandchild."

Now the management of the entire estate was in my hands. Neither Mother nor Corito had any interest in doing it, but they were clever enough not to entrust Camilo with more money than he needed for his peregrinations. Mother's interests were her garden and her mah-jongg sessions. Although not greedy, Corito turned out to be a perennial source of pain in the coming years; her jealousy was such that it was best for me to stay away from Sta. Mesa. But that did not help much. She also grew quite stout. We had such violent quarrels we often came close to wrestling. We were very careful, however, never to quarrel in front of Angela; in fact, it was my love for Angela that brought me back to Sta. Mesa again and again like some masochist returning for more punishment.

Father's demise in orgiastic beatitude was to be replicated by Mother, but in a differently pleasurable manner. Her passing was described in detail by Doña Petra, her mah-jongg companion of many years. For several sessions, Mother had had no luck, and, being impetuous, she had increased the bet so much there was now a lot of anxiety at the table. Then, it happened—for once, she was truly lucky and when she ecstatically cried, "Pong!" she slumped forward in victory and death. Like Father, her heart stopped.

Just twenty-four and I now had to manage all our properties. It should have been Corito, she being older and better educated and all that, but she devoted her time to Angela, who was, even at birth, very sickly. I feared she would not survive. Corito almost died, too, when Angela was born. She had to have a hysterectomy and the fact that she could never have another child made her care all the more fastidiously for her only child. Corito's condition, among other things, bound me to her no matter how much I loathed her afterward.

7

Nationalist entrepreneur! How I loved to be called that. I emblazoned it in my mind, the best accolade I have received. But a sense of humility—my friends would call it rare and out of character—informs me I should lower my self-esteem a bit. I did not start from the bottom, so to speak. I did not struggle against fearsome odds. From the very start, position, power— they were all mine to use and all I did really was to be clear-headed and logical in reaching for more of the same. For this reason, I am hesitant to narrate my entrepreneurial conquests, if they may be called that. I did not sweat to achieve them and though I pride myself in being here—the summit—it is in the more personal triumphs that I glory, the acquisition of a rare book, or an old Philippine painting or antique, the discovery of an excellent menu and, most sensually satisfying of all, the total and dearly sought acquiescence of a woman.

Forgive me then, dear reader, if I bleat not about my business skills. Bear with me instead as I take you with me into this mysterious and pleasurable domain called woman.

But I am dying. My thoughts, then, should not be acrimonious and bitter. I should be filled with Christian charity, not demanded by religion but by an inner compulsion. I want to be remembered as one not miserly with his affection. This is the inviolate truth. My excesses can be explained by my love for life, maybe my own, and also for those to whom I am devoted.

I am dying, and even with all my resources, I am powerless to stave off death. Is my condition now the supreme irony? Did God will it or some unfathomable fate? To be imprisoned in a useless body, to have the mind alert, capable of memory and cunning but not able to command the body to act—is this punishment? In spite of my iron Catholic upbringing, in my most decrepit condition, now I questioned Him. If He is such a perfect Being, why did He create an imperfect world, why was He miserly when He denied perfection to men? A Jew who converses with God would reply: so man can make his own moral choices. Why must such a choice be made at all?

Father had shown me how important political ties are, not so much because with politics we shape the state but because with politics we preserve and enlarge our power base. I am sure this was also an almost instinctual knowledge he had inherited from my grandfather. He was always close to those who wielded power and he himself belonged to that anointed circle which some Filipino writers, jealous of our discrete and durable privilege, have derisively called the oligarchy.

My own generation had quickly matured, was made cynical even, by the war. But we were not old enough to take over when that war ended. Being entrusted with the care of our properties, Corito and I being the only heirs, I merely continued in the first two years what Father had done, buying up as much land as possible in the expanding suburbs of Manila, particularly in Makati. As Grandfather said when our Sta. Mesa house was being built, the city will surely overflow its present boundaries in an untidy sprawl. One did not have to be prescient to foresee that.

I did better than both. Before I was thirty, I had looked keenly at the economy with a vision sharpened by those days in college, by my contacts with classmates whose parents were achievers. Now I went into banking and insurance, and, with an eye ever to the future, much of it encouraged by my early visits to Japan, I went into shipping. At twenty-six, I was truly a taipan.

At this time the reparations from Japan were pouring in. I was not going to miss my opportunities. My interest in Japan had developed from those conversations with the Japanese officers, particularly with Colonel Masuda. I am sure that he died in Leyte, poor man, for if he were still alive, he would surely have surfaced in Japan. A man with his academic background would be most useful to the Americans.

Now, shipping. I have often wondered why there weren't more Filipino industrialists who became shipbuilders. I am only too aware of the archipelagic nature of our country, the need for a strong navy and a maritime industry. I know, of course, the basic reasons—the absence of a steel industry, technical people capable of building engines, metallurgists, ct cetera. Such efforts can only be initiated by government working hand-in-hand with industry.

I go back to our history, to our past as a seafaring people, to those magnificent galleons that crossed the Pacific in epic voyages, and how we have trained thousands of seamen to man the world's ships.

It was not on a whim that I went, therefore, into this enterprise. So let me say again that I have contributed what I can.

I started with the interisland routes that have always been profitable. With reparations, I was able to obtain three secondhand but still seaworthy ferries from Japan. I wondered how they could be altered into passenger boats—at the time, there was not enough technology in the Philippines. I looked around at the shipbuilding industry that was then starting in Korea—and there I took the three ferries to be refitted, modernized. It took them a year, and when I brought these ships back to Manila for the southern route—Cebu, Davao, Manila—they turned out to be the grandest ships that ever sailed the Philippine seas.

It was just a matter of time; my shipping department was managed by a young tyro whose father was a former executive of Compaña Maritima, the old prewar shipping line. He was mestizo—you guessed it—and extremely able. When he was ready, we went international, with first four tankers to service the oil needs of the Philippines, then container ships—they were coming into vogue—for the Pacific ports and Japan.

I would gladly have built those ships in the Philippines, but we did not have the facilities. Japan had become too expensive—the Japanese could not compete with the Koreans—so all the new ships were built at the giant shipyard in Koji.

Now they are complaining about how expensive shipping costs are. Manila to Seattle is cheaper than Manila to Davao. But of course! We have banded together—a cartel, our critics would call us. We are merely maximizing profits, taking what the market can bear. What do those bleeding hearts, those weepy do-gooders expect? A free ride?

I did not see Korea during the Korean War, but I saw pictures of that country as it was ravaged by that war. All those mountains that surround Seoul were bare rock then as were those mountains all the way down the peninsula. Not now—they are all caparisoned with trees, no easy achievement in less than two decades.

On my third business trip to Seoul, to the shipbuilding company's main office, I met Choonja. It matters not that her family name is Kim, millions of Koreans have that family name, or Lee. She was the secretary of the executive vice president who was personally attending to my requirements. Choonja stood out in that austere conference room where she was taking notes. She reminded me almost instantly of Adela, except that she was very fair, with brownish hair, and her eyes—they were much like Adela's, dreamy and pensive.

I had brought along a dozen of my people, my accountants, my engineers, including an American consultant. The president of the company attended the first hour of the meeting, but he left soon after. My own presence really was not all that necessary, for my staff knew what to do. We were hammering out the final agreement and the meeting was tiring because we were looking at so many details. Thank God this beautiful executive secretary relieved the tedium. Our eyes often locked, but she would quickly return to her notes. Looking at her, I hurtled back to another time with nostalgia, remorse and then pity, for Adela had surely perished in the battle for Manila.

That first day ended with relief, particularly when the Korean vice president said we would attend a *kaesang* party that evening. It was the first time I had ever heard about the *kaesang*. And Miss Kim explained to us that the *kaesang* is what the geisha is to the Japanese—an official entertainer. Miss Kim made all the arrangements and our host was no other than the company president. From our hotel that evening—the new Chosun—we were taken in limousines to the outskirts of Seoul. It was dark, so I couldn't see where we were, other than that we seemed to be going up a hill. Then we were before a brightly lighted building, the Blue Cloud Restaurant.

It was autumn, late October, and Korean autumns are chilly but lovely in the daytime when the sky is unblemished and pure. I remember very well that persimmons were already in season, and peonies were in bloom, splotches of lavender and violet in the parks where Choonja took me.

One thing about the Koreans: they do not indulge in obscure euphemisms when they entertain. They said outright that we could bring any of the girls who served us that night back to our hotels.

The food was exotic but hot, the usual kimchi, raw fish, barbecued beef. Eight girls in their dainty Korean dress performed a fan dance, and an athletic but lithe girl, lovely even with just the slightest makeup, danced, all the while beating two drums in tidy precision. The party broke up at ten, early enough so that we could hurry back to the Chosun before curfew, retire early and get ready for the grueling session the following day.

My boys waited for my cue; knowing that they wouldn't bring any of the girls with them if I didn't take one, I did bring with me the girl who sat at my side and tried to make me comfortable during the dinner. She spoke some English—she was about twenty or so and was heavily made up. In my suite that night, she washed her makeup off and I was surprised to find her even prettier. I asked why the heavy cosmetics, and she said so she would not be recognized when she went to the Blue Cloud. I asked if she knew how to massage, and she said she did, and that was all she gave me. Exhausted, encroached by tedium, I soon fell asleep. When I awoke in the morning, she was already in ordinary street clothes. I wanted to take her to the dining room for breakfast but she said she would rather go home, that is, if I no longer needed her. She also had school to attend. I had abstained, I am sure, because my thoughts were on Miss Kim. I think she was worried that I wouldn't give her any tip and was truly grateful when I gave her a fistful of won—she embraced and kissed me noisily.

At the conference room that morning, Miss Kim greeted me with a knowing smile. "I hope," she said, "you had a wonderful time last night."

"Thanks to you, yes," I said, winking at her. She seemed embarrassed, and turned away quickly.

Again, the same tiring procedure. Before we recessed for lunch I told the Korean vice president I would like to go shopping that afternoon and, looking at Miss Kim, I said I hoped she could join me for lunch so that we could proceed from there.

The Korean was bewildered, but he could not refuse me, of that I was sure. After some harried conversation, he said, bowing, "Yes, Miss Kim can go with you."

As we headed for the elevator, she was grim-faced. But only for a while. Finally, in the lobby, she burst out laughing. "He couldn't say no to you; I am glad you took me away from that meeting. It is hard work for me, too, and he said it would be difficult to get someone from the staff to do what I was doing. I hope you won't repeat it."

I assured her that I certainly would.

Then she asked what I wanted to buy.

"Nothing, really," I said honestly. "I just want to be with you. To look at you. You are so pretty and you remind me so much of my youth, of a girl I was in love with, who really looked like you. Your eyes, particularly."

"You did not marry her?"

"I am a bachelor."

"I know," she said. It occurred to me that the Koreans are very thorough, that they study the background of the people they deal with.

"She died during the war," I said simply.

"I am sorry," she said. "So many tragedies happen in war. My family is in North Korea—I have no word of them. I fled here with my grandfather when I was a child. . . ."

We went to a cozy restaurant in nearby Myung Dong and had barbecued eel, fragrant rice, raw fish and the inevitable kimchi. She wanted to call for one of the company limousines, but I told her it would be more fun if we went by ourselves and took whatever transport was available. I learned she had gone to Ewha College, which was exclusively for girls, and that was where she took up American literature, primarily so she could master English. She lived in Chongro-ku, a district in the city itself, in a small apartment with her grandfather. She was earning good money, she said, and she was glad she had taken up

literature, for not only did she learn English but most of its id-
ioms as well.

We had an argument when she said her favorite American
novelist was Faulkner; I said he was difficult, inscrutable, af-
fected, prolix, extremely self-indulgent and confused in his
thinking.

She laughed. "You just have no patience," she said. Then
she asked me who my favorite was and I said, "Hemingway."

It was her turn to lambaste me. "He is simple, too direct, too
mannered, too choppy, and his prose is trite. . . ."

We let it go at that. She decided to take me to Itaewon.
"That is where many foreigners go," she explained. "Particularly the American soldiers. There is a lot of variety there,
mostly goods for export—the foreigners say it is cheaper but,
actually, it isn't—there are places cheaper than Itaewon but
these are frequented only by us, and they are not as colorful as
Itaewon."

When we got there, I had already convinced her to stop calling me sir or Mr. Cobello but to call me Charlie instead.

She agreed, but would do so only when there were just the
two of us. In the presence of her boss, and my people, she
would always be formal.

Itaewon was like a dry-goods supermarket. Both sides of the
street were lined with boutiques selling sneakers, jackets, fashion dresses, army surplus and, between these shops, the usual
restaurants serving American fare. A lot of foreigners, many of
them apparently GIs, were in the shops and on the sidewalk.

In the leather shops, jackets and coats made to order were
priced way below what they would cost in America or Europe.
We passed a fur shop with soft, shiny mink coats and jackets.
Choonja said many foreigners buy Korean mink because it is
the cheapest in the world. The Koreans were now raising the
animals in farms and were breaking into the world market just
like they were doing with their many consumer products.

We walked in. I had bought Corito a sable coat in Stockholm last year, her second, and she scolded me because not only did she not have much opportunity to wear it but it seemed to her a useless expense. My mother's lessons on frugality again.

I asked Choonja to try one, which she immediately did—a full-length silver mink. She looked at herself in the mirror and smiled. "I can daydream, can't I?"

I had decided even before she put it on. "It is not a daydream, Choonja. It is yours."

She grinned. "You must be joking," she said, taking the coat off and putting it back on the rack.

"No," I said. "Put it on and walk out of this shop with it. And have your old woolen coat wrapped up."

She realized then that I was serious, ready to part with a small fortune for a girl I barely knew. But that's me, impulsive with women, and gallant to a fault.

"No," she said, angry now. "I won't permit it."

I looked at the salesgirl, her face now saddened. She knew Choonja was rejecting my gift. Choonja spoke to her in Korean, but the woman simply smiled and replied in what seemed like words meant to placate her.

"What is she saying?"

Choonja turned to me. "She thinks you are my husband, and how lucky I am to have such a rich husband."

Then she laughed and I laughed with her. "I cannot accept it, Charlie," she finally said. "Thank you for the gesture, I know you really want to give it. And I know you can afford to give away a hundred of these. But look at me. How will I explain this to my grandfather? How will I explain it to the people at the office? I don't earn that much, you know."

"No problem," I said. "When I get to your office tomorrow, I will tell your boss I bought you this coat in appreciation of your company."

More arguments, but she realized that I really wanted to give her the coat. And when she went to the office the next morning, she wore it. And at the meeting, I told everyone it was my way of expressing my thanks for Miss Kim's company.

After dinner, before we parted for the evening, Choonja was pensive. "No one has ever given me a gift this expensive," she said. "I suppose you expect some form of repayment?" she asked, laughter in her eyes.

"No," I said, and meant it. "I do not expect anything, just your companionship, or your friendship."

She asked me when I would leave Seoul.

"When you want me to," I said.

It was she who asked me to stay on, which I decided to do. The next day, after my boys had gone to Koji in the south to visit the shipbuilding facilities—I had been there six months earlier—and, from there, home, she came to the hotel to have breakfast with me. It was Saturday and she did not have to work.

I did not want to appear overly amorous, so I said, "I have yet to look at the antiques shops. I have a few pieces of Silla pottery . . ."

Her eyes brightened. "So you are interested in our past, too," she said.

"I am interested in antiques, yes," I said. "But I am more interested in the present, its challenges and possibilities."

"We must go to Kyŏngju then," she suggested. "That is the old capital of Silla. And that may be where you can find some beautiful stuff. Although you may not take it out. There's a government edict against that."

We left soon after in a hired car; a new highway stretched from Seoul all the way to the port of Pusan in the south, and the railroad to Pusan, too, had been improved to take on express trains. We passed several cities and towns, their names familiar to those who knew the Korean War—Suwŏn, Ch'ŏnan,

Taejŏn. The fields were amber with the rice harvest, and within the yards of the new tile-roofed farmhouses, the persimmon trees were laden with ripening fruit. We reached Kyŏngju shortly after midday and had lunch in a new hotel. We spent the afternoon driving around, visiting temples that wouldn't register in my mind, my attention claimed by this magnificent creature sitting beside me. We paused in a couple of antique shops where I did buy a celadon vase and a bowl at her suggestion. We dined on the hotel terrace overlooking the ancient city, talking very little, my mind focused on how it will be, the sweet expectation.

That night, alone with her in my suite at last, she teased. "This is what you want, isn't it?"

I said yes. I was honest. "But I didn't ask for this, please keep that in mind. I gave you a gift, gave it with all my heart—and that's it. Thank you, my dear Choonja, for being with me tonight."

That night was a disaster. I couldn't explain it. Here I was, expectant, all revved up, healthy and mentally primed. She was all that I imagined her to be, her skin so pure, like cream in the light. At twenty-one, she looked much younger, a girl in her late teens. We had kissed with passion, and she was all ready, and so was I but when the moment came, I couldn't do it!

The following day, I tried to analyze my failure. She said I was tired, perhaps my mind was on business all the time. How did I perform with the girl from the Blue Cloud Restaurant?

"She just gave me a massage," I said. She did not believe me.

We went that Sunday to P'anmunjŏm where the Armistice was signed, the North Koreans on one side of the 38th parallel, the South Koreans and the Americans on the other side. It was the first time for both of us; the trees had grown and cranes had built their nests in the trees. There wasn't really much to see—those grim North Korean faces, barbed wire and men ready with their guns. It was depressing, and it was so good to be back in Seoul. That evening, we went across the Han and had dinner in one of those restaurants on its banks. I was told that some of the restaurant patrons purposely went across the river at night; in the event that the North Koreans attacked, they could be in Seoul in a matter of hours. Those across the river would then be able to escape the first waves of invaders. But we went back to the hotel, my last night in Seoul, although, of course, I could stay longer if I wanted to.

Again, the same frustration that had so angered me and curdled my mind. How could it be? And then, I realized, it was perhaps because Choonja reminded me so much of Adela. That was the most logical explanation. When she left me in the morning, after we had slept embracing one another and enjoying the warmth of our bodies in the autumn cold, I told her what I suspected was the reason, the profound obstruction in my mind, my memory of Adela still very much alive in my heart.

That night, I dreamed, too, not of Adela but of Severina. I was young again and so was she. We were in the kitchen at the cook's table eating with our hands, just as I used to, enjoying the honest simplicity of the servants' peasant food, rice fried with garlic, strong Benguet coffee and thick strips of salted fish and sliced, ripe tomatoes. In my dream, I found Severina more beautiful than Adela, than Choonja, and I could swear the food tasted better than any I have had in those gourmet restaurants.

8

I n Manila, I often dialed Seoul knowing Choonja would have to clear the call. I had nothing important to say, I just wanted to hear her voice. She would laugh gently, knowing the truth, and if her boss was not around, we would talk at length. In this way, I learned of her engagement to one of the company's engineers a year later.

It was January and cold in Seoul but pleasant in Manila. I asked her to spend her honeymoon in the Philippines and I sent her two airline tickets so she wouldn't be able to say no. They were met at the airport by my travel people and brought to the Dasmariñas house. I gave a small dinner for them that evening and invited the Korean ambassador and his deputy chief of mission who, as it turned out, had been the groom's classmate at Seoul National University.

Choonja was in a pastel green cotton dress and her cheeks were pinkish with youth. I didn't pay much attention to her husband, but I did have a brief conversation with him to make him feel comfortable. He knew about the mink coat—in fact, her whole office knew about it, and they had considered her very lucky indeed. And now, this honeymoon trip. I sent them to Baguio for a couple of days, then the yacht took them to Palawan for a week of fishing, lolling on the beach and snorkeling. They returned to Manila sunburned but happy.

On their last Sunday, the deputy chief of mission took Choonja's husband for a game of golf in Marikina. They were to be there the whole day and, in the evening, the classmate was giving a dinner for them.

"I will see to it that Choonja is entertained," I assured him.

I took her to the Club for breakfast, then we motored to Tagaytay. We reminisced on the way, and I held her hand, which she did not draw away, her hands so soft, the fingers tapering, her nails clipped and unpolished.

My visit to Tagaytay also enabled me to look at the real estate I had bought there—three hundred contiguous hectares, some on the plateau overlooking the lake and the volcano and extending across the national highway. All of this would someday be developed as either residential area or intensively cultivated farms, planted to vegetables not possible to grow in the lowland heat.

As we ascended the plateau, Choonja noted the perceptible greening of the land although the rainy season had passed. On both sides of the road, interspersed among the coconut palms, were low papayas, rows of daisies, and pineapples. It was the first time Choonja had seen pineapple plants. They were far sweeter, I told her, when picked ripe, unlike those that were exported to her country and to Japan—pineapples from Hawaii, harvested while still unripe.

We passed a long stretch of fallow land—all of it mine—that was to be developed soon. Again, I got all of it cheaply by adding credibility to the well-known reputation of this region as bandit country, plagued by many unsolved murders, and that many of the earlier landowners were forced to leave because of threats from these "bandits," some of them in my employ in my security agency.

I had support from the public officials who stood to profit because they knew that Cobello y Cia would eventually come to the rescue of this desolate land.

At the time, I had not yet built a house in Tagaytay; that would have sent the wrong signal to upper-class Filipinos who appreciated Tagaytay's climate and isolation from Manila, a scarce thirty miles away.

We drove over to the old lodge that had been built before the war. As we neared it, Choonja gasped in awe and wonder: to our left, like some blue mirage, Taal Lake suddenly appeared through a screen of grass and trees, glittering in the noonday sun. At its center rose the green cone of the volcano.

"It is beautiful," she murmured.

At the lodge grounds, I took a picture of her standing against the ledge that overlooked the lake. She wore a sky-blue ramie dress that I had asked Christian—Manila's best couturier—to make; had she been in Spain, I would have asked Balenciaga to design a few dresses for her. She brightened the frame—she would be photogenic; even in closeups, that beauty would shine through.

We went to the lodge coffee shop. We just had coffee, then went to the Mercedes and drove back to Manila. She dozed in the car and I put an arm around her. She leaned on me, her fragrance swirling around me. I had wanted to ask her about her husband then, but I did not want the driver to hear an intimate conversation.

Now, all my drivers—in fact, my entire household staff—are discreet and trustworthy. And my drivers are also trained mechanics and are my bodyguards as well, experts in the martial arts, fully armed and skilled marksmen. I don't believe in going around with a platoon of bodyguards; just one, well trained and loyal, will do, particularly since, I am quite sure, I have no real *atrasos*—that is to say, people who would really want to do me in are few and wouldn't have the determination and courage to do it anyway.

As we neared Manila, she woke up, and realizing that my arm was around her, she snuggled closer. I had remembered only too well my Seoul misadventure, my disastrous failure that certainly lessened my self-esteem. I wondered how she had felt on those two nights that we had embraced, both of us anxious, and I couldn't do it! I had never felt such humiliation before, such a damning sense of impotence, and thinking back, I was thankful for her expression of sympathy rather than ridicule, how she had kissed me so tenderly, as if such expression of affection would banish the bone-deep anger and frustration that shriveled me.

We returned to the penthouse.

While the cook was preparing our lunch, we drank some red wine in the living room.

It occurred to me then to ask about her husband.

"Did you enjoy Baguio? It is quite cool there."

She smiled and nodded.

Without warning I asked, "Is he a good lover?"

She looked at me quizzically. "I don't understand," she said.

"When he made love to you, did he please you? Was he good in bed?"

Again, that impish smile. "Charlie—I really don't know. I never knew any man other than my husband. In fact"—she leaned over, held my hand and pressed it—"you would have been the first . . ."

For some time, I couldn't speak. I finally said, a knot in my throat, "I am very sorry—oh, not for you, but for myself . . ."

She leaned over and kissed me on the cheek—no insinuation of passion, just a simple, domestic kiss.

A leisurely lunch on the terrace, Korean barbecue—prawns,

thin strips of beef and chicken—on the brass brazier I had brought back from Seoul, and the kimchi she had not forgotten to bring. When it was over, I asked her if she wanted to nap—my bed was ready. But she said she was not tired. I took her to the bedroom. We were now alone and I kissed her. She responded, but her kiss was sterile, a habit.

I let go, then told her that I wanted to take her portrait, to which she gladly acceded, knowing that I enjoyed photography.

Let me again be immodest and say that some of my best pictures would be envied by Cecil Beaton and my portraits can equal if not surpass those of Richard Avedon. I had been taking pictures since before World War II with those simple box cameras and, afterward, with the more sophisticated models from Germany and, after the war, with the first Japanese imitations of the Leica and the Contax. Some critics have pointed out that my reputation as a photographer is enhanced by my being rich. That even with my expensive equipment, most of my pictures are lifeless. They have perhaps seen only my still lifes, not the portraits and the other "living" pictures I have taken of anonymous people at their chores. Yes, I have a roomful of cameras, including those antiques that are still serviceable and the latest models including the Japanese electronic geegaws. But people do not normally know how hard I work in the darkroom, sometimes the whole night when I have taken some pictures that I think are experimental or great. The darkroom! That's where pictures are created, and the photographer who does not know a developer from a fixer is a phony. There are men of means who call themselves photographer-artists but have never been inside a darkroom!

We went to the game room with the skylight; it was meant to be my studio as well. I lowered several screens for background and positioned the strobe lights and the shades. I posed her seated on a sofa, standing by a wooden pillar, holding a rose. These being over, I said I wanted to photograph her in the nude.

For an instant, hesitation clouded her face.

"I have seen you twice in your glory," I said. "I want to record that. Are you ashamed, Choonja?"

She smiled and said, "No. But this picture, only you will see it?"

I assured her so. I showed her the file of nudes I had taken, all of them under lock and key, the safe where the negatives were stored. "You can keep the negatives if you wish," I said.

Again, that beatific smile. "Will you tell my husband?"

"That is your decision."

"No," she said firmly. "He does not know anything."

She started peeling off her clothes; her skin much, much fairer where the bathing suit had covered it. It would make a stark contrast, particularly since I was photographing her in black and white. Seeing her thus, my throat ached, the blood in my ears thundered. I had to wait a little for the welts on her skin made by her bra and panty to disappear. I took a bottle of lotion from the shelf to apply to portions of the skin that seemed shiny and, as I touched her, I could feel myself coming to life at last. I embraced her then and kissed her with passion. For a while she clung to me, thrusting a leg forward so she could feel my manhood audaciously, unashamedly proclaiming itself. Then she pushed me away, gently. Her voice was tinged with sorrow and regret when she said, "I am sorry, Charlie. But I want to be faithful to my husband."

I did not persist; I understood.

That evening, after I had delivered Choonja to her husband, her virtue intact, I returned in haste to the penthouse and worked frenziedly in the darkroom till long past midnight. First, I developed the negatives with utmost care, dried them, then made contact prints. I have always been partial to the Hasselblad; its square format simplified composition. The negative is also sharper. The Leica's has more depth. I then enlarged the portraits—this took the longest; I made fourteen-by-nineteen enlargements, a dozen of them. Eagerly, I waited for the images to form in the developer. There was Choonja, finally, the shy smile, the lips half parted as if she were teasing me, the eyes brilliant as usual.

It occurred to me then to bring out the other portraits of the women I was most attracted to—half a dozen who had graced my bed, and half a dozen more who would have done the same had I persevered beyond disrobing and photographing them. I ranged the portraits around the studio, against the walls, perched them on the sofa, on the writing desk. Then I turned on all the floodlights and, slowly, like a gourmet surveying a splendid buffet table, I regaled myself with that luscious variety. I studied all the faces, mostly Asian with a bit of Caucasian mix. A black-and-white photograph is more exacting, more precise in character delineation because it is bereft of the cloying exaggeration of color. The starkness of truth prevails, probes through the fine gloss of the lens and beauty glitters in its purest essence as expressed by the eyes. The eyes! I went around again and finally came to Choonja, and nostalgia suddenly came crashing over me like a mighty surf; poignant tears started to mist my vision. The eyes, yes, the eyes! These were what had attracted me to all of them and all had magic—mysterious, brooding, deep—in their eyes, the same eyes as Severina's that had beckoned to me through all the years. I knew then it was not these women, and in the future, not Ann or Yoshiko, loved though they were, for whom I had pined and ached and truly cherished. It was Severina all along, the girl of my youth whom I had wronged!

Thus endeth another melancholy chapter of my life.

⚁

I started visiting Japan in the fifties as my enterprises developed. Indeed, Japan was poor, its population hungry and with the peso at two to a dollar, the exchange rate being 360 yen to the dollar, every Filipino who went to Tokyo at the time was a profligate prince. I stayed at a hotel near the Imperial Palace, the Nikkatsu and, sometimes, in the afternoons, when General MacArthur left his office nearby, I went there to watch him, as did many Japanese who wanted a glimpse of the man who now ruled them. He had been to our Sta. Mesa house several times and had even talked with me; had I greeted him and reminded him of those dinners in Sta. Mesa I am sure he would have remembered. After all, it was also he who signed the commendation that made my father a colonel in the U.S. Army! But I contented myself with one of his senior aides whom I had also met in Sta. Mesa and, once, the general did pause when we met in the corridor by his office and said hello, but he was too big to bother with a young businessman from Manila.

To millions of Filipinos and to the now docile Japanese, he was more than ten feet tall; indeed, he was physically impressive—that stern jaw, that wide brow, that heroic stance—they were theatrical, they endowed him with glamor and charisma. But looking back, he was an ordinary mortal, loyal to his friends in Manila. I would not be surprised to find out that Father had introduced him to a couple, maybe a dozen even, of beautiful Manila mestizas while he lived in the Manila Hotel. If all those guerrilla records were to be believed, then Father had served his country well in spite of his pimping for the Japanese and serving in the Laurel government. He was never brought to trial for collaboration, unlike the others—that was their luck, a result of their inability to understand the primordial rule for survival: create personal bonds with those in power; pander to them. Human beings that they are, they will reciprocate.

I was to hear soon after the war the reason for MacArthur's cozy relationship with the mestizo elite. Quezon gave him half a million dollars in 1942, when the dollar was still so highly valued. How much would that be worth today? This rumor, which percolated widely, would soon be confirmed by historians. Indeed, we Filipinos are not only grateful and hospitable to our friends—we are also very liberal with our spending of the people's money. Collaboration then, and its stigma, was not perceived as a moral issue, only political. But that was soon settled when many of the collaborators ran for public office and got deluged with so many votes, when men like my father—bless him for his wisdom and his prescience—and my grandfather, too, not only maintained their social status but also strengthened it vastly. I was absolutely sure, therefore, that when the dictatorship would end, those of us who pandered to the Leader would remain anointed with power and social position.

Soon enough, those bleeding hearts who believed in American justice would ask why MacArthur decreed land reform in Japan and not in the Philippines. Simple! He had no friends among the *zaibatsus,* the Japanese financial conglomerates. In the Philippines, we surrounded him, pampered him, then smothered him.

Ah, the Tokyo of my youth! There were no jets then except in the military, and the four-engine, double-deck Boeing Stratocruiser took almost the whole night to reach Haneda. On my first trip, I left Manila close to midnight and reached Haneda in the early morning. There was no airport building in Manila then—just a simple shed at the end of the runway. Outside the airport in Haneda were mudflats, wide open spaces. Tokyo was still very much a city of the low wooden buildings that had survived the fire bombing by the Americans. The Korean War was winding down to a stalemate and the P'anmunjŏm peace talks had started. Tramcars clattered in the main avenues and *soba* boys, one hand supporting a tray of noodles, raced through the crowded streets with miraculous agility. Most of the nightclubs were provided with music by Filipino bands. In fact, Filipino musicians were in many Asian cities before World War II. I have told this story often, how I entered the nightclubs in Tokyo in the fifties with eyes closed, ears keenly tuned to the music and, after a minute or so, I would know for certain if it was a Filipino band playing. The Japanese played Western music perfectly, cleanly, each note in place. But their music, though precise, was cold, without feeling. Not the Filipino bands. They played with that deft human touch that showed that not just the intellect and the hands were making music, but the heart was, too.

These sorties into the nightlife were the major attraction of Tokyo to me then; I was young, virile, with all the lust for living. Yoshiwara, that old and famous red-light district of Tokyo, was still open, the brothels lining the streets, wooden houses with their young women, some of them newly arrived from the rural areas, seated in their fronts and flaunting their youth and innocence. There were more tourists than guests.

Yoshiko was not from Yoshiwara. She worked at the information booth of Takashimaya, one of the department stores at the Ginza—a huge stone building that seemed to have survived the war. She spoke passable English at a time when there were very few who could speak the language. I had asked her to escort me when she was off duty and she had agreed, primarily, I think, because I had offered her quite a sum for a day's work. She was tall, but not as tall as me, and slim. In her store uniform, with her hat and all, she looked trim, and prim.

It was much, much later that I developed temple and museum fatigue. But in my youth, I visited them all avidly, noted every curio and all minutiae; the manicured gardens, the architecture, the use of wood and beams—the major characteristics of Japanese architecture.

I should see Nikko then, Yoshiko suggested.

Japanese department stores even then were well stocked and a delight—I learned it was at Takashimaya that the Emperor's family shopped, so I concluded it must be loaded with quality goods. Indeed, even at this time, when Japan was poor, imported consumer goods were already available in specially designated places; one could easily recognize these places because their floors were carpeted. I had bought a brand-new Nikon from the tax-free shop across the street and had left it at the stationery counter where I had purchased some handmade paper. I did not even realize I had left the camera there until I heard the announcement over the speaker system that it was waiting for me at the information booth on the ground floor. Talk about honesty and service; even to this day, I am sure, both are not in short supply.

That was where I met Yoshiko. When I presented myself, she looked me over, then, after a while, she smiled. "Yes, you are the owner."

She told me later that the salesgirl at the stationery section had described me as tall, fair-skinned, about twenty-five or so and very handsome.

She was off at seven when the store closed. I did not tell her I wanted a date, but five minutes before seven, I was at her counter, asking where the best steak house was. She said she knew of one in the next street that served Kobe beef, very expensive and frequented only by businessmen. Would she like to have dinner with me? She demurred at first. Just dinner, I asked in my best pleading manner, and she finally agreed.

It was fall, the lights of the Ginza were on, the drooping leaves of the willow trees that lined the street shimmering and silver. It was cool, and not used to the cool weather, I had a topcoat on. She had a thick black sweater over her uniform, her cap now in her bag. She was, of course, made up as all the salesgirls in the department stores were made up, but it was easy to see that Yoshiko was beautiful even without all the powder, rouge and lipstick.

You must remember, this was in the early fifties, when a pack of Camels was enough to obtain a lay. Oh, those were the days when Japan was a playground for many Filipinos, and glib as we are and used to flattering our women, the Japanese woman who had always been regarded as inferior was so easy to seduce. Besides, then as now, they suffered no moral inhibitions about fucking—they would gladly do it for the sheer pleasure.

Yoshiko turned out to be different, indifferent to the best seduction techniques I knew. After dinner, we went to one of the nightclubs along the Ginza where a Filipino band was playing and where Bimbo Danao, a mestizo, was singing. I had known Bimbo when he was in Manila crooning during the war in one of the Escolta theaters. Shortly after Liberation, he had migrated to Japan, where he was getting much more money and attention from the women. I sought him out to impress Yoshiko, and for her he sang a Japanese love song.

I took Yoshiko to the Nikkatsu, where we had hot *soba*. I tried to get her upstairs to my room, but she said she had to hurry and catch the last Yamanote train to her home in Ikebukuro.

It was my first experience of being rejected by a Japanese girl at a time when they were easy conquests, and I was baffled and, for the first time, too, doubted my capabilities. I looked at myself in the mirror—a tall man with patrician features, a noble brow, a sensual mouth. I wondered if she did not like my hotel. It was not as classy as the Imperial nearby, which I did not like. Although designed by Frank Lloyd Wright, a famous American architect, its lobby was tiny and dim and certainly did not conform to the Japanese architectural dictum. I decided to move there to let her know that I had means. I also decided to stay a few more days—I was not worried about my business; at the time, I had already learned certain basics, like selecting good people, paying them well, delegating authority and axing them if they fumbled.

On the day that Takashimaya was closed, I don't recall now which weekday it was, Yoshiko consented to take me to Nikko, this fabled shrine up in the mountains near Tokyo. We took a train at Asakusa station and, in a couple of hours, we reached the town, then up a zigzag road to the temple itself. She was no longer in her store uniform. She was wearing a blue wool suit and, over it, an old black leather coat. Patches of snow lay on the ground and I made a couple of snowballs and threw them at her; she did the same. We were enjoying ourselves and laughing. She had explained to me on the train that she had studied American literature in a Jesuit school, which explained her knowledge of English. I missed it all, the ancient cedars that lined one of the narrow roads that led to the shrine, the gorgeous temple bedecked with a surfeit of gold filigree, much more elaborate than any church altar I have seen. Everything simply flitted by my vision although I was not in a daze. On that perfect autumn day, alive with sunshine and the dazzling colors of leaves, I could only look at this splendid girl. How I longed to possess her.

I was prepared to spend that day and night in Nikko—there was no shortage of hotels; in fact, some of them were precisely for couples on a binge—but it would not be. She said we had to return to Tokyo. At the Asakusa station, she refused to go to the Imperial, chiding me for having transferred from a very good hotel to this snobby place frequented only by Americans. No amount of pleading could convince her to have dinner with me, but she did kiss me, almost as an afterthought, when she left me there, dumbfounded, mystified and horribly frustrated. I stood bewildered on the platform long after her train had left.

The riddle of Yoshiko was settled a year later, but this is going ahead of the story. I was back in the Ginza soon enough, and hoping to see her, I went to the department store at closing time. She did not see me, and it was just as well. She was walking out of the store with a big black American woman in uniform—probably a WAC—and they were holding hands.

9

I am now leaving the straight chronology of time because this digression that I am relating happened almost two years afterward, during which time I came to terms with what is afflicting me. I would have never known of it had I not been frustrated by Yoshiko that day. That discovery has, since then, made me conclude that even in adversity, there is yet some good to be found.

I had returned to Tokyo to finalize negotiations with Marubishi—the powerful Japanese trading company that was interested in going into partnership with me. It had survived MacArthur's edicts against the *zaibatsus* and was now enlarging its operations, eager to make connections in Southeast Asia.

Let it be known that Yoshiko's rejection did not totally faze me. Nothing ever seems to defeat me—like that doll with a lead bottom, you can knock it any way you like but it always bounces back, upright, because it was made to be that way. It is with this attitude that one enters into business with the Japanese. How does one really do it? A Filipino would have no difficulty, unlike the Americans, who have such poor empathy with the behavior of Asians; in a sense, that is what the Japanese are, although they are loath to admit it, looking down as they do at all Asians, but not at the Americans nor the Europeans, to whom they feel inferior.

As I said, it is like dealing with Filipinos. A lot of sake has to be consumed and even when they say they will try, that is certainly not definite, not till the relationship is bonded, and then the Japanese word is as trustworthy as the yen. But again, *cuedao*—because they are pragmatic and unyielding when it comes to what they perceive as ensuring the survival of their group.

By this time, too, I saw the absolute necessity of learning Japanese. I bought several Japanese-language records, and whenever I had the time, I had Commander Martinez come up to talk with me in the language. He was a former naval intelligence officer who had mastered the language, could read and write it, and was one of my top executives. I always brought him to Japan when there were important negotiations. I had asked him not to speak Japanese at all in the presence of the Japanese we did business with, but, being very thorough, they must have known of his background. I am sure, though, that they were unaware of my adequate proficiency in their language, which I never used with them. I have been tempted so many times but I have always desisted. No, as we Filipinos say, they cannot sell me down the river. Knowing that I did not speak Japanese, they often made comments concerning me, nothing derogatory at all, just remarks that I may be hungry, or tired. I did not even use it when talking with Yoshiko; in the first place, there was no need, as her English was adequate.

I have mentioned that one of my top executives is Commander Martinez—not a mestizo, really, but with skin fair enough to pass for one. He came from the Ilokos where, for sure, those itinerant Agustinians must have fertilized the region with their genes. He would have rotted in Camp Murphy then, pushing papers, because he had angered a politician close to the Palace.

But first, my rationale for him. With a huge organization—more than twenty-five thousand personnel—I do need a kind of security force that can check on my people as well as protect me and my enterprises. What would be the best source of such trained people if not the army itself? And more specifically, the graduates of the Philippine Military Academy. How did I come to this conclusion? Simple—I had my planning staff study the structure of our armed forces, how decisions are made, who makes the decisions. It soon became obvious that, as in all large organizations, cliques exist, competing with one another for scarce resources. The most powerful cliques were dominated by graduates of the Military Academy, strategically located in the different branches and in different ranks—all of them bonded by personal ties arising from when they were cadets living together and sharing the adventures of young manhood.

This is going ahead of the story, but years afterward when I was assigned to South America, I realized the great difference between our armed forces and the Latin American armed forces; there, the elite corps is drawn from the continent's elite families. There are no oligarchic names in our officer corps, no Cobellos, Danteses or Rojos. Almost to a man, they are all Indio.

From the very beginning, therefore, I made it a very important objective to recruit retired officers, and even those on active duty who could be enticed. That is not difficult because most of them are paid so low, and with Cobello y Cia, almost immediately after they leave the service, they get more than double their measly government pay, not to mention the fringe benefits and the prestige of working with an established institution like mine. After an officer gets to be a captain, the rise in the ranks is painfully slow and this is the time when it is easiest to lure them away from military life. No, I never aimed for the brightest in the corps; the most popular cadet in his time is the best. First, he knows how to work with people, else he would never have been the most popular in his class. That is not all—keep in mind that if you have one man from each graduating class of the military academy, you have a key to the entire army network, for the army is no different from other Filipino institutions. Those relationships developed in college will come to good use in the future, and, in a sense, this is how I endeared myself to the military; this is how they have also protected me and my interests.

In the freezer for six years, Commander Martinez used the time to learn Japanese, German and Spanish, all of which were put to use when he joined Cobello y Cia.

I had some difficulty reeling him in—a big fish like Martinez is an instinctive fighter, his skills as such honed during the war years when he was a guerrilla. A senior at the Philippine Military Academy in 1941, he was inducted as officer immediately at the outbreak of hostilities. He escaped from the Bataan death march and immediately joined the guerrillas.

How do you hook an Indio who had amply illustrated his patriotism with deeds and not with inane gestures as I have often done? How else but show him that these gestures are not meaningless, that they bespeak the best intentions which, if they are not actualized, would yet be when hindrances to their realization were removed.

As part of that indoctrination process, I took him to the Sta. Mesa house to show him the library, the preening collection of Philippine antiques. Where possible, I also brought him to my charity missions for the ethnic groups, showed to him my interest in Philippine culture by being supportive of all its creative aspects. No explanations, no rationalizations.

If later he had doubts, I allayed those with excellent pay and fringe benefits and, most of all, with trips abroad wherein he was often a glorified valet but nonetheless anointed by his seeming closeness to me. I knew I had won his complete loyalty when he asked me to stand as godfather to his youngest son, whose employ in Cobello y Cia I had assured him.

So here I was in Tokyo again to pursue not just the yen but a luscious information clerk at Takashimaya. Midsummer, but it never really gets very warm in Tokyo. I did not want to meet the black woman who, I was sure, would be waiting for Yoshiko when the department store closed, so I went there in the morning, at ten, when it opened. She was as beautiful as when I first saw her, and it seemed as if she had not aged a day. She was extremely pleased to see me—that much I could elicit from the warmth with which she greeted me, the lingering handclasp. I asked her when her day off was—it had not changed.

"Let us go to Kyoto," I said.

She shook her head immediately. "That is so far, Charlie"— she remembered my nickname. "We cannot make it in a day; the trip alone would take half the day."

The other salesgirl was listening and I could tell that Yoshiko did not want her to hear our conversation. "I will pick you up when the store closes," I said. "And we can have dinner together."

I was a little surprised when she said quickly, "Yes, that would be fine." So her lover wouldn't be coming for her after all. Maybe Yoshiko had already ended the relationship. Many things could have happened in the past year, maybe the other woman had been reassigned or sent back to the States. I was eager to find out.

I had some difficulty getting away from a business meeting, and also avoiding the usual evening ritual of going out with my associates for a round of drinks. I thought she had already left, for I was twenty minutes late and, in Tokyo, because of the excellent public transport, there is no excuse. The big stores at the Ginza had closed, but not the boutiques. The taxi stopped right at the main entrance and she was there, maintaining solitary vigil. She accepted my explanation graciously, she had some knowledge already of my business interests but did not seem awed by them.

We took the subway to Shibuya and had dinner at Peco, a small Italian restaurant in Nampeidai; she had been to it only a few times and she said it served the best pizza in Tokyo; the crust was indeed fresh and crisp.

The Japanese, like the Chinese, are not demonstrative. They seldom hold hands in public, but I held her hand just the same as we walked back to the train station. Had she already taken her vacation?

"What is that?"

It was almost unknown in the Japanese labor system. She was happy with her job, and she would most probably hold on to it for as long as she wanted, until perhaps she got married.

So, she had some feminine ambition after all.

"And raise children?"

She nodded.

I was very pleased to hear that, to know she was not all that much of a lesbian. It was July, and Tokyo was unusually warm. She had taken off her blouse and underneath was a yellow T-shirt that revealed her shoulders, the fine down at the nape of her neck. Shibuya even then was alive with young people, the small shops bursting with goods. We passed several love motels, I was holding her hand, and I said how wonderful it would be if she would consent to go to one of them with me. She stiffened and withdrew her hand. I was not joking, of course, but I made it sound as if I was. "What is the matter with you, Yoshiko?" I asked, sounding hurt. "Can you not even take a joke? And why are you so scared of men? Of me?"

"I am not," she said resolutely.

"Then come to Kyoto with me," I said. And that was when I offered her so much for the trip, what she perhaps earned in six months she would make in three days. "You will be my guide, that is all. Nothing more . . . I promise."

She was quiet after that. Then she said that when she was a child, her family had lived in Shibuya, in Nampeidai—they had a house with a garden and a couple of persimmon trees that bore so much fruit in the fall they had more than enough for the neighbors. But after the war, they had to sell the house and land to get a much cheaper and smaller place in Ikebukuro. "My mother is with me, Charlie. She is not well and I am taking care of her. One reason why I cannot leave Tokyo for so long . . ."

We reached the Shibuya station where she would take the Yamanote train. She took me to a statue of a small dog facing the station plaza. "This is Hachiko," she said, patting the dog's head. "Wait for me here Sunday morning, very early—at seven o'clock. Yes, I will go to Kyoto with you. I have never been there either."

I opened my briefcase and gave her a wad of ten thousand yen notes without counting it. I asked if it would cover our tickets, and she said it was more than enough. She started counting but I stopped her. "Just keep it and tell me if it's not enough."

"I will make a list of everything I spend," she said.

⌘

Even before we started for Kyoto that early morning, I had already planned what to do. She was waiting before the statue of the dog when I got there fifteen minutes early, which was usual with the Japanese. We'd have time for coffee as she had already bought our tickets and made the reservations at an inn in Kyoto. She was in a light blue summer dress and was carrying a weekender canvas bag and a plastic bag that she said contained our lunch and iced tea. We went to one of the coffee shops across the square and had coffee and toast. She had had no breakfast, other than a cup of tea. She told me the statue's story:

Some time ago, there was this dog that went to the train station every afternoon to meet its master. Then one afternoon, the master failed to show up—he had been killed in an accident. The dog stayed on, waiting, waiting. It did not leave the station till it died. Another of those beautiful Japanese stories that soon pass into legend.

"There are other popular waiting places," Yoshiko said. "The Ginza corner in front of Mitsukoshi department store or Waco—the jewelry shop—the ground floor before the escalator of the Kinokuniya bookshop in Shinjuku, almost all the train stations . . . but nothing as popular or as crowded as Hachiko."

I asked her if she would have waited for me much longer when I was late at Takashimaya, and she smiled beautifully. "I was willing to give you an hour. . . ."

I held her hand impulsively across the table and almost spilled the goblet of water before her.

The bullet train was yet to come, but the old trains were roomy and comfortable. The countryside, bright with sunshine, slipped by, rice fields just planted, tiny, tidy Japanese houses, the farmers' homes easily identifiable by their thatched roofs. Orange orchards, dark green in the sun and, always, in the distance, mountains or, up ahead, a succession of tunnels.

It is unusual that I can still remember these scenes for, in truth, during the trip to Kyoto, Yoshiko's presence dominated my awareness: the manner in which she spoke, her gestures, all that serene beauty, inflaming my imagination, how her pristine composure would change in the unrestrained throes of passion.

Four hours to Kyoto, four hours that seemed no more than six minutes afterward. She told me about her life, reticently at first, then with confidence as she went on. I was, of course, a good listener.

"I told you about our house in Nampeidai," she said. "It was really beautiful. I am very sorry we lost it, but it cannot be helped. My father—he was an engineer. They made him an officer and sent him to China. That was where he was killed. The war. And my two brothers—they were older. I was only a little girl then. They were both studying at Keio University. They were drafted into the army and sent to Okinawa. They did not return."

The lilt in her voice was gone; her eyes had misted.

"You don't have to tell me these things, Yoshiko," I said. "I know what war is like. . . . Remember, we were occupied by your soldiers."

She turned to me. "I have heard they were brutal, that they made people in the occupied countries suffer so much . . ."

I simply nodded.

She was silent again.

"My mother had to work, and shortly after I got out of school, I had to work, too. I never finished college, Charlie. We couldn't afford it, and our house now, I would like to invite you there—you are so good—but it is so tiny . . ."

I understood, realizing that my own Japanese partners seldom invited me to their homes. We always met at some classy restaurant or bar in Akasaka. Twice I did get invited, once in Chiba, and still another time in Meguro—substantial, middle-class-looking houses in Manila, but to the Japanese, they were manorial.

We reached Kyoto station in early afternoon, sweltering, hotter than Tokyo, and boarded a cab. The inn was by the Kamo River. Yoshiko, right at the foyer, objected immediately to the arrangements. I understood, of course, what was going on but I stood there dumbly, as if I didn't know a thing. She must have another room, no matter how small. But the receptionist, in a light blue summer kimono, explained that all the rooms were taken and, besides, what was wrong with being in the same room? We were such a good-looking couple, and it would be cheaper, too.

I asked what the trouble was, but she said it was all right, we would share the room.

"Oh, like an old married couple," I bantered.

She looked at me and blushed. "Not on the same futon, Charlie. And please, no jokes."

There was not much to unpack, and after we were through she called for a cab that would take us on a tour of the city. Temples, more temples, narrow streets and old houses of wood. I still never really paid much attention to them, or to the explanations she faithfully recited from the thick guidebook that she had been desultorily reading on the train. At dusk, with a surfeit of temples, I wanted to have dinner in any of the restaurants listed in her guidebook—a restaurant that specialized in Kyoto cuisine. But she said breakfast and dinner were provided by the inn, and we were not going to waste money.

We went back and realized that the inn was truly full—more than three dozen girls in blue school uniform were there, noisy as a flock of ducks.

"Senior high," Yoshiko said. "A very exclusive girls' school in Tokyo."

We had dinner in our room, served in those beautiful lacquered trays, tiny portions of pickled vegetables, fish, rice and what else—the food so neatly arranged, like carefully executed pictures, it was a shame to eat it.

After dinner, we went out again. I wanted to stay in our room, to be with her, but she said the night tour was already paid for and, besides, she said with a mocking smile, it should interest me because it included a tour of the entertainment district, and we would see some old-style Japanese courtesans.

"Whores," I said under my breath.

"What did you say?"

"Never mind," I said.

The tour bus was full. As I looked around, I was surprised to see that I was the only foreigner. Some noisy old ladies, and quiet old men. Yoshiko had brought along her guidebook and translated what the tour guide said. The evening tour was for Japanese only, and Yoshiko said it was authentic, nothing touristy about it. I let everything bounce off my consciousness, interesting though it was, the geisha quarters, the *taiyu*—that was what the courtesan was called—in a kimono with the sash worn in front, her traditional wooden clogs almost six inches high.

We returned to the inn shortly before midnight. She had enjoyed herself, seeing that part of her society that was shut off to so many Japanese.

The maid had prepared the bath and she said I should bathe first.

"Why don't we bathe together?" I asked.

She smiled. "No." She was firm. "You first."

I did not soak in the tub, stayed only long enough to melt the tiredness in my bones.

My futon was a meter away from hers and I was tempted to draw them closer but desisted.

I was almost asleep when she emerged from the bath and, in a short while, she lay down, too, in her summer *yukata*.

"What will we do tomorrow?"

"Go to Nara and see more temples."

"I am fed up with temples," I said.

"The tour is already paid for."

There was no avoiding it. "I would like to see some interesting places," I said. "Like bars where homosexuals go, both men and women."

"Not in Kyoto," she said. "I don't know any place here. But we can do that in Tokyo. I know a couple of places there."

"Are there a lot of homosexuals and lesbians in Japan?"

"I don't know," she said. "Why do you ask?"

"Just curious," I said. "I do not condemn them—if that is their choice. Me, I have always preferred women."

She chuckled. "I know."

"And you?"

She mumbled something I couldn't understand. I didn't ask her to explain.

Nor did I tell her that I had seen her and the black woman holding hands. Maybe I was wrong. But I did tell her that women who turn to lesbianism do so because they have never experienced a man's embrace, that once they have had that experience, they would never seek sexual pleasure again from women.

"That is the entire difference," I said. "As for men, it could be a different point of view and there are, to be sure, men who are ambivalent—AC/DC we call them in Manila. They usually make good hairdressers, couturiers and even artists."

After a while, she said she was sleepy; we could talk about it some more in the morning.

I turned to her; she had closed her eyes. Although there was no light, the evening glow filtered into the room and I could make out everything clearly, the low lacquered table where our meals were set, the cabinets, the scroll and the vase with artificial silk chrysanthemums. The faint mustiness of the tatami mats pervaded the room, some lingering fragrance of Japanese incense; from our right, through the shuttered window, the murmur of the river as it followed its course, some giggling from the girls in the other rooms. I was not sleepy, I was not going to sleep—I had plans and would soon act on them.

Past midnight, the whole inn was quiet. Yoshiko had not covered herself with the sheet. The fan at one corner of the room was not on and it was no longer warm; in fact, it was quite cool. I did not rise—I merely crouched and crawled over to her side. She was breathing rhythmically, quietly, in her sleep. I bent over her and kissed her gently. When she did not wake up, I kissed her again, this time forcing my tongue into her mouth. She woke with a start. I think she knew at once it was me but she did not push me away. Her eyes were now wide open, but my eyes were more used to the darkness. I spoke to her gently, quietly. "I am going to rape you, Yoshiko. You can struggle and scream any way you like, I do not care." I meant every word. I held her wrists and mounted her, my *yukata* open at the front. She had nothing on under her *yukata* and, soon enough, her breasts greeted me. I bent over and kissed them, then kissed her again.

She finally spoke. "I should not have come with you," she said. "Do what you like, I am not going to scream—what is the use?"

But though she did not struggle, I could feel her body stiffen. With anger? With tension? I was in no hurry. I decided to put her at ease first. I started the old ritual, caressing her, petting her until I knew she had relaxed completely and was even enjoying my ministrations.

I mounted her then and, cooperative at last, she spread her legs. Perhaps I was too anxious, but I slipped in slowly, glorying in the feeling of being welcome. And when I finally fully entered her in one quick thrust, she screamed, *"Itai!"*

I had thought that it was sheer pleasure that had elicited that cry. She tensed again.

"What did you say?"

"Ouch," she said, translating what she had uttered. It occurred to me then to ask, "Is this your first time?"

She nodded, her eyes closed. I did not move for a while. I kissed her instead. Now she responded with passion, her tongue probing my mouth. When she was finally relaxed, I started moving again, slowly, and, at first, she lay still; then she picked up the rhythm of my exertions, and she began thrusting her hips upward to meet me. She soon started to moan, and embrace me tightly, and I could feel the spasms, the contractions, but I went on pumping steadily. Her back arched; and when she came, she let out a cry that I am sure was heard in the other rooms. I did not stop, and again, her moaning, her wild embrace . . .

"Yoshiko," I said, "you are very noisy."

"What did you say?" She was oblivious to the world. I could only think of the high school girls in the other rooms, all of them awake, all of them listening eagerly, and I said to myself, To hell with them all.

We went to sleep in a leechlike embrace and were awakened by the maid, who wanted to serve us breakfast. I looked at my watch—it was past ten! There was no latch to the door. Yoshiko said we would have breakfast later. She embraced and kissed me. "Thank you, Charlie," she said, her eyes shining with gratitude.

I kissed her hungrily. "This is the breakfast I like," I said, mounting her again and, once more, those moans of pleasure which, by now, I had become used to.

The morning sun caressed our room, sparkled on the shoji screen and brought a sheen to the red lacquered table. Exhausted, Yoshiko lay on her stomach, her face half-turned toward me. Her eyes were closed as in sleep but she was awake, her lips parted in a smile of full contentment.

I moved closer to gaze at her profile. Such sweet repose. Her hair cascaded on the other side, baring her nape. I'd read somewhere how Japanese males regard a woman's nape with its fine growth of hair as an object of erotic admiration. I immediately understood.

Her back glistened in the morning light, the graceful curve of the spine, the narrow waist, the gentle humps of her buttocks, and those sculpted limbs tapering from her flanks. A woman cannot see her back, the buttocks that darken a little as they slope into her thighs. The skin is coarser here, the pores bigger, but with Yoshiko, it was clear, smooth as peach skin.

Of all Asian women, it is perhaps the Japanese woman who has the most beautiful skin, so unlike that of Caucasian women; it is only when they are in their teens or early twenties that their skin is tightly drawn and smooth. But as Caucasian women age, their skin thickens and is rough to the touch, particularly where there is an abundance of skin hair. The skin then becomes lax, flabby and coarse. Not that of Oriental women, least of all the Japanese woman. And her complexion—they commingle there: the orchid petal, the polished ivory, the pink pearl.

I turned Yoshiko over. Slowly, she lay on her back, revealing that ineffable glory, that face in full dulcet symmetry, those luscious lips slightly parted. I leaned over and kissed them. She responded warmly enough to tell me she was, indeed, fully awake. My finger wandered down the graceful line of her jaw, to the soft fall of her shoulders, the hair in her armpits. She shivered a bit when I bent over to kiss them, exuding not that odor of sweat for which reason many Western women shave. It was the lifting aroma of a woman, wholesome and newly scrubbed.

I licked the creamy mounds of her breast, traced with my tongue the light red aura that encircled the nipple, darker and rigid now in my mouth and tasting of honeyed salt. My tongue wandered down to her navel and, below, the brown patch of pubic hair, so soft, so downy, at my touch. A quiver, a tiny moan, then she sat up to enfold me in her arms.

▨

When we finally got up, I noticed the specks of red on her *yukata*. I pointed them out and she smiled. "It was painful only in the beginning." She did not bother to wash it—the maid would probably think it was her monthly and not the immaculate evidence of what she gave up for me.

The three days in Kyoto became a glorious, impetuous week; we went to Nara anyhow because the tour was already paid for, but we did not finish it; halfway through, when wandering around the deer park, we slipped away from the group and headed for the train station to Kyoto, just in time, for the girls in the other rooms were trooping in. They looked at Yoshiko and me impishly and with knowing smiles, which, at first, Yoshiko could not understand until I explained to her. Again, one of those beautiful blushes reddened her face, even her ears.

On the train back to Tokyo, we talked with an openness that was refreshing, for now she unveiled her innermost feelings, her fear that she might get pregnant. Abortion was legal, though, and that was one recourse she could take if . . .

"Don't, Yoshiko," I said, although I was sure that I could no longer get any woman pregnant. "If you should ever be, I will marry you. Raise the child—after all, it is ours . . ."

She held my hand and pressed it. "I will think about it," she said. She then went on to tell me that there was a time, her father had told her, when baby girls in Japan were killed by the parents if they were poor. Thinning out, they called it.

Was she bothered by the fact that she was no longer a virgin?

Again, a blush bloomed on her face. Then she said quickly, "No, it does not matter so much. But if it did, the Japanese surgeons are so good, they can restore the broken hymen." Then she said she had had to quit her job—her extended absence necessitated it. But, with the money I gave her, there was enough for her and her mother to live on until she found another job. She assured me it was not difficult to find one in Tokyo.

I was now sorry and felt responsible for her plight. I told her I would try to get her into Marubishi—I knew some of their top people. Otherwise, she could always come to Manila where she could work in one of my companies.

It turned out that her father had worked for Marubishi, in

their heavy industries division. Why, then, did she not seek employment in the company? "Simple," she said, "I did not know anyone."

It was not difficult to get her a position in Marubishi; some of the biggies there remembered her father. I left Tokyo very much elated. Not only had Yoshiko gotten a good job but most of all I had weaned her away from a deviation that would have psychologically maimed her later. Although she never admitted this, I could sense her gratefulness. She came to Manila with her ailing mother the following year, and they stayed in Sta. Mesa for a couple of weeks. The day before they arrived, I sent Corito and Angela on a trip to Europe. Yoshiko shared several days with me in Baguio, in Hong Kong, then back to Tokyo.

When she got married, however, she cut off further relations with me. For her wedding, I gave her an emerald set—earrings, necklace, ring, all from Wako, and a superb *poulownia* cabinet for her bedroom. On occasion, she would send a card, or if I was in Tokyo, she would call and ask how I was. That was how it should end. I had no regrets.

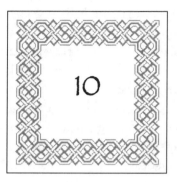

10

But to return to that early evening the previous year when Yoshiko dumped me in Asakusa after our excursion to Nikko. I was in no hurry to return to the Imperial, lonely and frustrated as I was. I walked to nearby Yoshiwara—the Japanese closed it soon after. I wandered, dispirited, around the old rickety prostitution quarter, the teahouses glowing with their paper lanterns, the girls seated out front in the autumn cold, dressed in their woolens, some of them in winter kimonos. I entered several teahouses but did not linger long.

I finally saw her—demure, dainty, my quintessential image of a Japanese beauty and, having made arrangements with the madam, she soon changed into ordinary Western dress, over it an olive green U.S. Army winter jacket. We took a taxi to the Imperial, which was quite a distance away, and held hands. Reiko—how can I forget her name? She spoke a little English, probably learned from her GI customers. She carried a small Japanese-English dictionary to which she often referred.

It was as I expected her to be: expertly passionate, solicitous, ever ready to respond to my every wish, even perhaps to perversions which, fortunately, I did not have. She waited for me to wake up in the morning and when I asked her to have breakfast with me, she said that she had to go, that is, if I did not want to do it anymore. And, of course, I did it again.

I left for Manila that noon. At the time, there were so few passengers flying, it was not necessary to make reservations. In Manila, in the late evening, the first symptom struck—an itchiness in the groin that worsened into a dull ache. I slept fitfully that night and in the morning I had difficulty urinating. When I finally did, to my surprise, pus was in my urine. I knew at once I had caught my first case of gonorrhea. *Qué barbaridad!*

I went immediately to our family doctor. Dr. Avecilla told me not to worry. Penicillin, he said, would kill it in a couple of days. He was right, but I wanted to be sure there were no bugs left in my system, so I told him to give me a blood test as well. He called me frantically the following day to see him immediately.

Dr. Avecilla was part Chinese, with chubby features and eyes that disappeared into mere slits when he laughed. His demeanor was humorless. "You have syphilis," he said without hesitation.

I was stunned. Wasn't the pencillin working?

"It would take more than a two-day treatment," he said. He went on to say that I must have had it for years and it was now in an advanced stage, which meant it would be more difficult to eradicate. He asked if I had noticed anything wrong with my body functions, any recurring ailment bothering me, but I was as healthy as a water buffalo. He said syphilis was a great imitator: it took on the symptoms of other diseases and it may have already damaged my body without my being aware of it.

He asked if in the past I had ever had a sore that did not heal quickly. And that was when I remembered: during the early days of Liberation, I did develop a sore on the lower lip that took a long time to heal. And I remember with some regret the exposures, to use his euphemism, in my father's brothel, with my dear Adela most of all.

"That's it!" he said, almost in triumph.

He gave me a book, as I wanted to know more about the disease. And as I read it, my heart slid down to the depths of melancholy and despair, fully convinced as I was now that I had brought ruin not just to myself but to my dear sister and our Angela.

When Corito delivered Angela, her womb, as I had already mentioned, was diseased and had to be removed. Angela, too, was sick from the start and I was filled with remorse that I was the cause of it all, not the sin that I had blamed earlier.

Would I now curse my father in his grave? And all those girls in Pasay? I never saw them again, not one, and I came to believe that, indeed, they had all perished at the Rizal Memorial Stadium. Or should I blame Colonel Masuda? It was he, I am sure now, who gave it to Adela, refusing as he did to touch her till the last night when Adela, in her ignorance, mounted him. In his refusal to touch her, I also realized how much he had cared for the exquisite prostitute, perhaps much, much more than I ever had.

How to face Corito now, to tell her the truth. We had never talked about it at length, but we had both blamed our sin as having visited our daughter; as long as she was alive and always in need of care, that was God's immutable way of reminding us of our guilt, for which there was no atonement, no absolution. Now, this sin was compounded by my youthful willfulness. I had brought perdition not just to my sister but to an innocent child as well.

I returned to Sta. Mesa in mid-morning; it was close to December, the weather was invigorating and cool and the rains had lifted. It was the part of the year when the garden was very green, when the blooms were shimmering red and yellow splotches on the ground and the sprays of violet orchids cascaded down from their wooden mounts. Corito was watering the orchids that Mother had loved, an interest she had inherited. She had put on weight now. Past thirty, she was heavy, with oncoming matronly bulges. She was in khaki overalls. I walked to her under the nylon netting that protected the vandas and the cattleyas from too much sun. Her brow was moist and we kissed briefly as we always did.

Where was Angela? It was a Saturday.

"Asleep in her room," she said. "She's not feeling well again. I will take her to the pediatrician in the afternoon." Angela was in grade four at the Assumption. She was pretty, as my offspring should be, except that she was so thin.

"I know now what is wrong with her, with you, too. And of course, me most of all. We are all sick, Corito. It is all my fault. I gave it to you. Syphilis."

She did not know what it was. I explained it to her simply. "Venereal disease." She dropped the water hose, squirting water on my face, my pants.

"No!" she cried. "No!" I held her as she shuddered and began to cry.

I dared not approach Dr. Avecilla about Corito and Angela. Manila doctors gossip although they are supposed to be discreet about their patients. Not only would he know that Corito and Angela were sick, but he would also quickly come to a conclusion about our relationship.

I did not care if it was still many days before the Christmas vacation. I had given so much money to those Assumption nuns that I could ask them anything. I rented a bungalow in Kowloon Tong in Hong Kong. Lincoln Road—a residential area, with a garden. I brought along three maids so Corito would not have to do any work. I bought a black Bentley and hired a driver. We were there for a vacation, and some medical consultations, for Angela most of all.

The gynecologist at the Anglican Hospital understood, perhaps, why Corito and Angela were being treated in Hong
Kong. She didn't ask questions other than what was required
professionally.

December finally. Hong Kong is lovely, cool and dry, unlike
the damp chill that often pervades Baguio at this time of year.
Those skyscrapers that now stud the Peak were just being built
and Kowloon was a warren of old brick buildings with antique
shops overflowing with goods from Britain and China, which
had been taken over by the Communists.

Confined as we were to a smaller house, we had a splendid
family life, and we motored often to the New Territories, to
the small immemorial towns where we dined in unpretentious
restaurants. I had to commute to Manila, however, getting
there in the morning and returning to Hong Kong the next
day, or spending a night there. Sometimes it was my people
who came over, for if there is one thing I have learned in business, it is to be on top of things, to ascertain the details even if
I left most of these to subordinates. I am systematic not just in
how I organize my time and my activities but also in storing
data in my mind and compartmentalizing decisions.

At this point, perhaps, my dear reader will wonder whatever
happened to Camilo, Corito's husband. The marriage was
never consummated because of his incapability. He knew Angela was not his, but he tried to make it appear to the public
that she was. It was his name, after all, which Angela bore. I
had the marriage annulled—yes, this can easily be done; for
what did I give all that money to Catholic charity? In time, too,
Angela's family name became Cobello.

Corito could take only so much; Camilo's ultimate insult
was when Corito caught him in her own bedroom with one of
the drivers. He was going to make a lot of trouble when Corito
drove him out of Sta. Mesa, and I did not want that. I talked
with him and, at first, he was adamant—he wanted a share of

Corito's wealth. I brought in Jake, my chief legal counsel (he was a classmate at the Ateneo), who then lectured him on the law, that he could not get a centavo if Corito refused. He had to accept my offer, which was quite substantial; it would enable him to live comfortably and even continue with his sexual proclivity. With the money, he set up a Spanish restaurant. I visited it several times and he greeted me affectionately, with the usual brotherly hug and all its innuendoes. He turned out to be a very good cook. His *lengua* is the best tongue in Manila.

But back to Hong Kong. In that month Corito and I abstained completely. I sometimes wonder if Angela ever suspected that I am her father, particularly when she grew older. When Corito kissed me, it did not appear as a sisterly kiss. I was often angry with her because she did it not just before Angela but before other people. It was her way of laying claim on me and such an attitude became a heavy burden for me to bear, especially when her jealousy became more and more pronounced. Since it was no longer possible for me to satisfy her insatiable hunger for sex, it soon became my very embarrassing duty to pimp for her. I use the word "pimp" categorically. It was I who paid her new sexual partners.

I did not leave Manila for Hong Kong without being sure my blood was cleansed. Massive doses of penicillin did it and, thank God, the disease had not yet developed resistance to the drug. Angela and Corito had three successive blood tests in Hong Kong before they left for Manila; I wanted to be sure about them, too. But as Dr. Avecilla said, even if it disappeared, it had already done much damage. The near future would soon reveal with unerring clarity how badly it had afflicted our bodies. I read that, in its advanced state, it damages the brain and creates those conditions sometimes defined as dementia. Have I been behaving erratically? If I have, my colleagues can always attribute it to eccentricity. Is there anything illogical in my thinking, buffoonery in my character? I doubt it. And if I am to be faulted, it will not be for my continuing high regard of myself, my crippling self-esteem, but only because I know I am surrounded by lesser men, by ignoramuses who have never scaled the heights as prodigiously as I have.

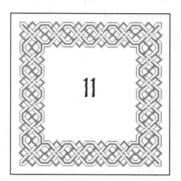

11

My stay in Hong Kong was not wasted; in fact, that month in the Crown colony opened my eyes to the business possibilities there, and in this I was ably assisted by Ann Lee.

I had experience by then in real estate development, and looking at Hong Kong, its central location, its sense of placid order sustained by the British, I knew it was an excellent place to invest in. I saw the owner of the bungalow we were renting and offered him a handsome price that he couldn't refuse. I also surveyed properties in the Mid-levels and still other properties in Kowloon. I wanted the old bungalow torn down and an apartment building erected on it, not a tall one like what I built later on in the Mid-levels; I needed an architectural firm in Hong Kong. It would have been easier to bring my people in from Manila, but I thought that if I had business in Hong Kong, I should get involved with the natives.

And that was how I met Ann Lee. Her father was a Shanghai tycoon who early enough saw the imminent fall of China to the Communists; so, as early as 1948, before they took over, he pulled up stakes and moved to Hong Kong with his whole family. When I met her, Ann Lee had just returned from the United States, where she had studied architecture and interior design. Immediately, we struck a congenial relationship that was to bloom soon enough, and would continue well into the future. She turned out to be not only loyal but also a good business adviser.

The architectural firm where Ann worked as a senior partner was recommended to me by the designer Hale Deller and the antiques dealer and interior decorator Carlota Hurstmann, names identified with the Hong Kong expatriate establishment. I met them at one of those ritzy parties in Manila. At first I found Ann a bit aloof, and this surprised me a little, particularly after I learned that she had studied in the United States. It turned out later, as I got to know her better, that this cultivated reticence was a kind of defense mechanism. It became her; she was tall and regal, with a classic cameo face such as those seen in ancient paintings of Chinese court ladies. She was rich, single and fair game for anyone with intelligence and charm. And these qualities, to be sure, were easily mine.

I picked her up from her Queens Road office and walked to the Star Ferry terminal where the Bentley—regal, black and shiny—was waiting. The Bentley was big. I would have preferred the Vanden Plas Princess, which was bigger and more comfortable, but it was not available and it would take six months for an order to be delivered. A Silver Cloud Rolls was suggested, but the Rolls was not my kind of ostentation; it was too common and everyone who could afford it could hire one. As a matter of fact, when Corito vacationed in Hong Kong before I got the Kowloon Tong house, she was always picked up at the airport by the Peninsula Hotel Rolls.

I had not meant to impress Ann Lee, but that really was what happened. "I see," she said pleasantly, "you have very good taste in motor cars."

Kowloon was not so crowded then with all those soaring

buildings, but Mongkok, which we passed, was where the masses congealed.

It was a perfect, unblemished November day. She was in her late twenties, with skin as pure as it was fair. And when she smiled, there was a dimple on her left cheek. Her English was American not English, as was the case with many of the Hong Kong Chinese, who were educated in England. I had met her only the week previous; I had gone to her office—one whole floor of the building—and was surprised to find the senior partner so young, and a woman at that. I did not know then that the architectural firm belonged to her father, one of several enterprises George Lee—that was his Christian name—owned in Hong Kong. He also had business interests in Singapore, Bangkok and Jakarta. One thing about the overseas Chinese, their network encompasses all of Southeast Asia.

I had furnished the Kowloon Tong house haphazardly; I had no professional help but, even so, Ann found it well upholstered and warm. When I told her I did the decorating myself, stuffing the house with odds and ends from Lane Crawford and Cat Street, she said that my taste was instinctive, probably acquired from my youngest days. She was right, for that was what had happened, exposed as I was to the genteel atmosphere of the house in Sta. Mesa.

I had told her of my plan to tear the old house down and build a four-story apartment building on the lot, each floor a single unit, with the top floor being mine. The rest would be rented out so that the house could pay for itself.

She could see at once the business sense behind it, although she was sorry that such a fine old house would have to be destroyed.

I told her I was interested in acquiring property on the Peak, and perhaps in the New Territories as well. Would she like to go into some form of partnership with me? Locate and help develop those properties?

She gave me one of those tentative smiles, then suggested

that we drive over to Taipo in the New Territories—she knew an excellent restaurant there, uncrowded, with something like home cooking. "My father is a gourmet," she said. "He found this place and we often go there."

It was high noon when we reached the Taipo restaurant, actually a ramshackle place crowded with working-class patrons. I did not know much about Chinese cooking then—Ann Lee's father introduced me to its variety and finesse afterward. She did the ordering, mushrooms and vegetables, noodles that were unusually thick and hot and fish head soup.

Sometime back, Tan, my Cantonese driver, had taken Corito, Angela and myself around the New Territories; he had explained the sights, the places we went to, but nothing of that short excursion was retained in my mind, nothing but the rice fields glazed with water, the walled-in villages, the small towns of brick and tile and the lotus ponds.

"After lunch," Ann Lee suggested, "since we are already here, let us go for a drive so you can see what this part of Hong Kong looks like."

The Bentley took the well-kept roads with agility and solid firmness. My Cantonese driver was also very pleased to be speeding out in the open. We drove close to the border, to Lok Ma Chau, where we could look across the fields to the mainland, to the guards in their towers in the distant hamlet keeping watch, herding China's millions home, at a time when so many had dared flee to Hong Kong, slipping through the barbed-wire borders, or swimming in the murky and open sea.

The drive also gave me an opportunity to tell Ann what I wanted to do, to have a Hong Kong base where I could have easy access to foreign and stable currencies. I asked her to be on the lookout for good property on the Peak; I wanted to build a condominium there, knowing that investments in the area would rise.

She came to Manila with her father in December with the plans for the Kowloon building, and they were my houseguests. Her father came, I think, to get a good look as well at the man with whom his daughter was getting financially involved. He did not have to come to Manila to check on me, he could very well have done that right in Hong Kong, but I am glad he did, for it was a real experience to know the man—urbane, educated in an American university, competent with his Mandarin and his English. He collected ancient Chinese porcelain, scrolls and other artifacts of traditional Chinese culture.

He looked over the collection of my parents and spotted two Sung fakes that, he said, would be very difficult to recognize unless one had developed a trained eye, and he showed me those telltale marks in the glaze that showed they were of recent manufacture. I went into the provenance of the items, and asked the Manila dealer to explain the forgery. Poor man, he had bought them in Hong Kong, from a Wanchai shop; he had kept the receipts.

When next I visited Hong Kong, George Lee took me to a bodega in Happy Valley—he owned a building there, several rooms filled with old china that could fetch several million dollars; then he showed me another room, also filled with china, but these, he said, were all fakes. He had been fooled not just once but many times, and he continued to be fooled, for it is difficult indeed to distinguish the fakes from the real stuff. His experience dampened my interest—I had thought that I already had a good eye, but after that day with George Lee, I knew I still had much to learn.

But back to Ann and her plans for the Kowloon property. At the time, I was also planning to do my Makati building.

"I met Naboku Tanga," she said, "when I was in college. He was teaching at Stanford and had already started building an international reputation. It would be great if you can have him design your building and whatever project you have in Hong Kong. I will speak with him."

I had reservations about working with architects who are

more interested in their ego trips than in doing what is right for their customers; I had a dim view of Frank Lloyd Wright's Imperial Hotel in Tokyo. I did not want the same experience dumped on me.

Ann understood me perfectly. "We will not permit that," she said with a grin. "We will redo the interiors according to our lights. We will just use his facade and, of course, his byline."

We went to Los Angeles, where Tanga had his main office. He was a small man with bushy eyebrows, and I could see that he coveted Ann. His lecherous eyes never left her all the while they talked and, on occasion, he would stroke her side, her arm.

Ann let him. It was easy for her to convince him to visit Hong Kong and Manila. He stayed for some time in the country, enjoying the Palawan beaches with Ann and dinners in Hong Kong with George Lee and myself. He was not going to charge me as heftily as he did the others because Ann was my partner, and he would do anything for her. I wondered if they had gone to bed together, but Ann had insinuated that Naboku Tanga was not her type at all, yet it was fun to flirt with him. He could be Japan's best contribution to the world of architecture, he could be one of the world's most famous builders, but he was a malleable ignoramus when it came to women.

I named the thirty-story condo on the Peak Angela Court, after my precious daughter. Thinking about it afterward, I think the name really fit in the sense that it is structurally fragile, like Angela, but this, only I, Ann and my structural engineer know.

The plans called for the laying of piles of the foundation at such and such a depth, deep into the rock, but I asked my structural engineer when a third of that foundation was already wedged into the ground if we shouldn't stop. Let me say that this was done at a time when computers were already widely in use. By his calculation we did not have to go so deep, as the minimum requirement had already been reached. The decision to go no deeper had saved us several million dollars. We really made a neat profit with Angela Court—even before the work had really started, just on the basis of plans, on Tanga's and Ann Lee's and my reputation; in the first six months that we were promoting it, all the units were sold. As usual, I reserved two units, one of them—the penthouse—for myself.

Thus stands proudly Angela Court, its steel beams criss-crossing, the hallmark of Tanga construction. From across the harbor, on the ferries, it dominates that portion of the peak—tall, preeminent, topped by the graceful sweep of a jukebox. And on those days when Hong Kong is festive, the Christmas season, the Chinese New Year, the building is lighted up in greens and reds, proclaiming itself with elegance and sheer sturdiness as it challenges the sky.

During the rainy season, however, I never stayed at Angela Court—it was always in Kowloon Tong. The reason is simple. A heavy rain could easily weaken the foundation of any of the buildings on the Peak and bring them crashing down. This had happened once or twice.

My Makati building, however, does not have this problem, for I had used structural steel as its skeleton; it is more expensive that way, but seeing those steel girders go up have put people's trust into the building itself—with Cobello y Cia, they cannot go wrong.

So there we were, Ann Lee and I working together, seeing each other every time I went to Hong Kong and being introduced as often as I saw her father to the finest concoctions of the Chinese kitchen. I had, in a sense, almost become a member of the Lee family.

Perhaps you will wonder why, from the very start, I was not attracted to Ann Lee. But of course I was, although not with singular passion, for while she was a beauty, she was also very businesslike. There were few occasions that her personal life intruded into our conversations. I did get hints, however, of a love affair in San Francisco during her college days that her father had not approved of. More than once, her father had obliquely mentioned that if Ann would get married at all, it must be to a Chinese who could contribute to the family's prestige—and, thus, I ruled myself out.

But it happened anyway, in the third year of our knowing each other and working together. Angela Court was all but finished and some of the units were already occupied. The penthouse was being furnished and the last carpentry touches were being done.

I remember it well—it was late Sunday afternoon, dusk, I should say, in April that we went up to the penthouse, she to look at what the decorators had done, and I to give a nod to whatever she wanted, for she had such good taste.

Some of the appliances had arrived, the big Hoover washing machine, the gas stove and refrigerator. No air-conditioning unit because the whole building was centrally air-conditioned. April in Hong Kong is balmy and that afternoon the temperature was just perfect. The sun was out washing the peak with silver and, across the harbor, the mountains of Kowloon were cobalt blue.

We had idled to the balcony, which was protected by a waist-high ledge; three stories below it, another patio surrounded the building, similarly protected by a ledge.

I looked down, and though we were high up, I said it was impossible to commit suicide from the penthouse—that patio three floors down would stop the fall and would result perhaps in a broken leg at the most.

"Do not talk like that," Ann Lee shouted—a shriek almost. It surprised me. She was never given to such sudden and emotional outbursts.

I reached for her hand, which she drew away. Her face was

grim, distraught, so I told her, "I won't do it, Ann. I was just making an observation. Jumping off any ledge is the farthest thing from my mind. I love life so much I would rather die of overeating . . ."

But the grimness in her face did not disappear. She went to the living room and sat on one of the chairs for the rosewood dining table that had come in. I sat beside her. "Now," I said softly, soothingly, "what did I say that angered you so?"

She turned to me after a while, her eyes downcast. "I will tell you a story—my story," she said. "Will you promise to listen?"

I took her hand again. This time she let me. Dusk was coming stealthily, and from where we were, we had a sweeping view of the harbor, the many ships that were now lit up and, across the water, the apartment blocks on Kowloon garlanded with light.

"You know," she began, "my father has this apartment building in San Francisco, at the other end of Chinatown, twelve floors, four apartments to each floor. One of the top-floor apartments was mine—I was living by myself, and it had three bedrooms. I drove to Stanford every morning. It was there that I met Glenn—he was taking up creative writing and was on a fellowship. He lived in a tiny room off-campus and did all sorts of things, clerking in the university bookshop, waiting tables at a Palo Alto restaurant. It was at the bookshop that I met him; we became friends. At first, I thought he was gay. He was slim, and there was also something effeminate in his movements. It was only later that I realized he was not gay at all, that if he kept away from dates and other forms of attachment with people, particularly girls, it was because he had very little money and whatever extra he earned he sent to support a sister at some institution for retarded people.

"I suppose, in the beginning, it was pity more than anything. But later on, I knew it was love. Mind you, we did it only once. Only once! And he lived with me for almost a year. I asked him to move into the apartment—there were two extra rooms and he could take either of them. He was hesitant. I drive to Palo Alto every day, I could leave earlier so he did not have to waste money on bus fare. And, afterward, he agreed. He did not have a lot—one suitcase, two boxes of books and a small radio. They all fit in the car.

"One night, he came home very late, long past midnight. I was awake and I could hear him in his room, moving about, so I stood up and went to his room. He couldn't sleep, he had received word from the institution where his sister was—she had died and they had cremated her body—they had asked him where the ashes were to be sent.

"I told him in China we keep the ashes in the family shrine.

" 'I would take it,' he said, 'and sprinkle it in that field in Nebraska where we used to play when we were children. I would have to make a special trip,' he said, and then he started to shudder and cry. I had to comfort him. I dragged him to my room, and that was when we did it. Just that once, but it was so memorable because he was so gentle.

"Then, Father arrived unannounced on one of his sudden trips to the States. He never stayed in the apartment, always at the St. Francis, which is his favorite. It was Sunday and I was at home, cleaning. He had a key, and there he was in the living room, his face contorted with anger, for he had seen the men's shoes there, and he started wandering around, opening cabinets, and was really very mad, particularly when he came across Glenn's clothes and things in the other room.

"I explained to him who Glenn was, and he said I was not going to live with an American writer who couldn't even afford an apartment of his own. He was leaving that afternoon, and he said I would have to return to Hong Kong with him.

"I am Chinese, a dutiful child. I hardly had enough time to write a good-bye letter.

"I tried to call Glenn from Hong Kong, but the telephone

in the apartment just kept ringing. I looked at my old address book. I called up the university bookshop. And that was when I learned that Glenn had jumped the day I left. But he didn't die, he was maimed, paralyzed from the waist down, and no one knew where he had gone.

"He knew my address in Hong Kong. I waited for a letter, any news from him. But all this time I have heard nothing. Nothing. And I remember all those times we had together, the tenderness—and then, I learned that he had died, that perhaps he had succeeded after all in ending his life."

She breathed deeply, then began to cry. Perhaps it was her story itself, her first time with Glenn, that was foremost in my mind. She sobbed aloud, the grief wrenched out of her soul with so much anguish, and I sat beside her, holding her shoulder, embracing her, but she didn't stop. Then I kissed her, her nape, her tear-washed cheeks. I undressed her slowly, first her blouse, then her skirt, and she did not object. Her sobbing diminished with the rising passion with which I caressed her. She was still sobbing faintly when we lay down.

The floor was dirty with plaster, with the leavings of carpenters. I had a copy of the *Hong Kong Tiger Standard*. I took off my blue cashmere blazer and laid it atop the newspaper. It was not all that comfortable. Years afterward, I used to remind her of this union, and she would look at me, laughter in her eyes, and say casually, in that pragmatic manner of the Chinese, that it had been good for the spine.

12

The Indios, nurtured by habits of docility and languor, cannot understand those among us who, burdened with eternal discontent, strive on, hacking away at our demons and, in the process, accumulating more wealth, more power. But even if these were attained, the discontent would continue to fester, to push and move us on. They think it is miserly greed that consumes our lives, and maybe it is, but it is also more than greed. It is achievement, to do battle not just with our peers but with our selves, to do much more than what was done yesterday. Remember the biblical story of the Tower of Babel? Behind much of human endeavor is an ideal, the writing of a book, the building of an empire, a reach for the stars, for God, whatever, there is an ideal, a goal, a purpose—maybe to give life meaning.

And the Indios are not handsome—a negative statement that avoids the direct and condescending view that they are ugly. I sit by the window of the Makati Cafe and watch the parade shortly after five, not the lower classes who seldom venture out of the alleys of Tondo and the slimy confines of the squatter ghettoes but the well-heeled middle class, the career girls, the junior executives with their silk neckties. I see them in their office finery as they go to the coffee shops and restaurants, to Rustan's to shop—the men in their gauzy barong Tagalogs, the traditional loose dress shirt, their paunches already prominent. In whatever dress, silks, linens or printed cottons, the women are often stubby and graceless, their faces like pancakes; as they themselves would say, a steam roller had lumbered over them. What do Indio faces remind me of? Pigs, monkeys, horses—animal faces with expressionless eyes. I walk out of the cafe when it is already quite dark; under the glow of neon and floodlight, their faces are now pale, funereal.

And what about myself? Certainly, in spite of my appetites, my idiosyncrasies, I would like to think this worthless hunk of flesh has given value to many things, to business, to progress, to the betterment of so many lives in my gainful employ. I have done well by my fellowmen. Just thinking about this gives me a sense of achievement.

If there is anything Indios cannot accept, it is the searing truth about themselves, their perfidious character, their ostentation and boastfulness. Who will believe their pronouncements, when everything is hot air, when no sooner have they proclaimed their virtue then they turn around and do the opposite? These Indios—they are stupid, and their country—thank God for exceptions like myself—is silly.

So here I am, high up on this pinnacle to which my wealth, my brains, my connections have catapulted me. High up, I can survey with disdain the old landscape around me, and way, way below, the masses—ah, the masses! They smell, you know, all this is exuded from their pores and it is loathsome as all bodily odor is. *Qué barbaridad.*

As I said, Corito and Angela had their blood examined three times. Angela wanted to know what was happening—I could not tell her the truth. I had told the gynecologist not to tell her. I said something about her continued weak condition perhaps being due to blood deficiency, and she believed it. She did not ask me again. We spent the New Year in Hong Kong—noisy with firecrackers hung from the buildings, but not as noisy as in Manila. After the New Year, we left Angela alone in the house and Corito and I registered in one of the new hotels on the island. Never again able to bear a child, she abandoned herself completely to passion and pleasure. I think that in the one day when we were by ourselves, I satisfied her.

I sometimes wonder why I never married. Was it because early in my life women had lost their mystique? Or was it because I knew I could never sire a child? Was my remaining a bachelor a token of my fidelity to Corito? But she knew I fornicated a lot, which, of course, she objected to. First, there were my beautiful nieces who vied with one another in seducing me, knowing that if they succeeded in dragging me to the altar, a great fortune awaited them. I was very kind to all of them. I would select from among them a companion when I went to the United States or Europe; their parents—my cousins—knew what was in store for them, but they did not seem to care. After all, when their daughters returned to Manila, although all of them had some measure of wealth, the girls were showered with expensive clothes and jewelry. I slaved at my business. Who would inherit my wealth? There was just too much for Corito and Angela. Why did I not share a little of it with them? Haven't they been very good to me?

Now I truly had freedom. Only the wealthy can understand this feeling. I knew, of course, the fullest extent of that wealth, the small details that matter. I was also aware of the strengths and weaknesses of my major people, my allies, the family names of most of my employees. I never called them by their first

names. This honor I reserved for the people in the highest ech-
elons, and for my closest friends. I tried to keep them all, even
those I regarded as my friends, at arm's length, never had them
close to my private life.

How wonderful that my father was close to Quezon so that
he was able to get huge chunks of Quezon City when that vast
estate was being divided. I added to that, much, much more
than Father had ever accumulated in his lifetime.

⬙

At this point, maybe it is necessary to explain why I am relating all this, delving into a cobwebbed past with memory already tarnished by age and disease. Some basic honesty is
demanded of me to even things out. But, perhaps, more than
this, I need to rationalize myself, justify even a past that enriched (and corroded, some would say) my life. I listen to my
own silent recitation of pious obscurities, the air wheezing,
rasping from my lungs and, above all, my own wind-drowned
call, begging Severina's forgiveness.

My illustrious grandfather died when I was a boy, but I remember him well and all those paeans to him, his monuments
in bronze—four of them, one in Manila, one in Pasay, another
in Caloocan and, of course, in Quezon City. These are his by
achievement. Now, this historian, Lamberto Campo, again; he
writes with Jesuitic elegance. He has mentioned my grandfather several times in his "new" history of the Philippines. He
insinuates brazenly that our wealth was ill-gotten from the beginning, that my grandfather had been left in the rear to take
charge of revolutionary funds. He married a wealthy woman
and used the money to buy huge tracts of land, enlarged further and legitimized by the cadastral surveys the Americans in-
stituted in the twenties. Grandfather and his wife were also
usurers; thus the Cobello fortune grew. The revolution was
lost, Aguinaldo was a prisoner. Would it have done any good
if Grandfather had handed all that money to the Americans?

This Lamberto Campo also alleges that my grandfather and most of the wealthy mestizos who joined the revolution when it was succeeding conspired to bleed this nation with a "development" plan that would have enriched them at the expense of the Republic. Again, I say: *Qué barbaridad!*

This Campo claims he has letters, documents and everything else on which his word formidably stands. Let him—no one can deny Grandfather's role in the revolution, and it is too late to alter all those history books, most of all, what had long been implanted in the minds of many generations of schoolchildren.

What is history anyway but soon forgotten and what remains are its pallid ghosts, the trite leavings as we understand them, confronted as we are with the demands of our daily lives. A street here, a phrase there, a footnote now and then, perhaps a memoir, an article—these are the reminders that do not really perish, and the so-called truths that this Lamberto Campo professes are only for those finicky worms in the libraries, those insignificant scribblers searching for bones bleached and flaking in cemeteries of the past.

But for people like me, history is a real luxury, for we have all the time to read, to amass the artifacts of the past, to contemplate this past if we are thinking at all. The people—those Indios who live in the farms, in rundown neighborhoods—to them history has no meaning. All they are aware of is us, the living with our sanctified names; we have been vested by history with the power to write it, create it, for that is what it has always been—history is written by the strong.

And who would now destroy what we have built through the years with our brawn, our entrepreneurship and our cunning? Not these puny rebel movements whose leaders we can buy. And as for those nationalist zealots, we can emasculate them just as easily with a government leadership cognizant of our power to co-opt their slogans, their heroes and mouthpieces. This should be clearly understood by those who seek power, who aspire to change the status quo or join it.

The playing field in the Philippines is never level and it is so wide open, anything goes. But why should it be level? When was it ever level? The regulations imposed by government do not mean anything if people in power are your friends. That is a major prerequisite, as I have always said. Know the people who matter. How I took over the Heritage Bank is instructive and it illustrates my point. I needed to have one in the early sixties—you cannot flourish in business unless you have a bank where you can store your money, a bank that you can use as a milking cow. I had a minority share in Heritage Bank and I wanted to control it for my own purposes. Increase its capital stock? And buy most of it? That is too expensive an operation, necessitating the tying up of so much capital that could be used elsewhere. Why not weaken the bank first, with massive withdrawals and the gossip that it is going to be bankrupt, innuendoes in the press—oh, that's the easiest thing to do, with almost all these journalists not only gullible but so easy to buy! Then, as it starts to stagger, as the stocks come in cheap, and with explicit threats of closure by the Central Bank, go in like the Lone Ranger to save it from disaster. And the depositors, not privy to your machinations, are even pleased that you are there at the right time!

▓

How fortunate that much of Hacienda Esperanza was planted to sugar and the major asset of Cobello y Cia is this and the sugar mill. Ah, sugar! The magic crop that is the foundation of my wealth and that of the Filipino elite. Sugar is thus also the foundation of Filipino politics.

Most Filipinos immediately associate the island of Negros and its effete and ostentatious *hacenderos* with sugar. They really do not know that the bulk of our sugar exports for the American quota is produced here, in Luzon. They are correct, however, when they say we were the most powerful economic group in the nation—the sugar bloc, why every Negrense, even with just a dozen hectares, wants to be called a sugar baron.

How fortunate indeed that, from the very beginning, my grandfather had latched on to this sweet enterprise, thereby assuring for my family not just wealth but political power. For those who are unfamiliar with sugar politics, a bit of background: the United States has traditional commodity agreements with favored nations. With us, it is sugar. Every American administration gives a quota to its clients. That is to say, if the world price for sugar is a hundred pesos a sack, for its friends, this price is increased to a hundred and fifty pesos—the additional fifty pesos to be shouldered by the American housewife. How could we sugar producers lose?

It follows then that it is necessary for us not simply to maintain this quota but to enlarge it, and we can do this only by pandering to American politicians, by being in their good graces. So we contribute to their political funds, pamper them with our unbeatable hospitality—they are, after all, only human.

We see to it therefore that every Philippine president is sympathetic to our interest. Ha! We have banded together to make our interest the national interest! It is not enough that our ambassador to Washington is himself a sugar man, a mestizo—we also see to it that every Philippine president is our man, sympathetic to our aspirations.

In mid-1971, the Leader called for me. I had carefully nurtured his friendship, having helped him in the last two elections that maintained him in the palace. He had once thought of making me a cabinet minister but I declined the position, for it would have overexposed me when what I really wanted was the embassy in Spain. I have always known that there was more Chinese blood in his system than Indio, which explained his cunning, his stealthy patience.

We were alone in his office, surrounded by all that shiny ma-

hogany. A little runt of an executive secretary was showing him
a batch of papers when I came in and he immediately dismissed
the man—he wanted us to be alone. I have always liked his
style—straight to the point, no time wasted. "Is Hacienda Esperanza doing all right, Carling?"

I smiled. "Yes, Mr. President."

He stood up, shook my hand and told me to sit down. "You
must convert more of your rice lands into sugar, and do it
quick. As for your rice tenants, make them immediately into
hired hands, laborers paid on a monthly or even daily basis. Do
this immediately, Carling."

"May I at least know the reason, Mr. President?" I was surprised by this unusual order.

He stood up, the visit was over, and as he walked me to the
door, an arm on my shoulder, he said quietly, "You are a very
dear friend, Carling. That is why."

A year later I realized the reason. He declared martial law
and simultaneously decreed a sweeping land reform program,
which, however, spared the coconut and sugar lands. All rice
and corn lands that were tenanted were to be distributed to the
tenants but not those rice and corn lands that were cultivated
by laborers on a daily, weekly, or monthly wage. Hacienda Esperanza was untouched.

How are noncareer Filipino ambassadors chosen? How else
but from the ranks of those who had contributed to the
Leader's coffers. I had always wanted to be ambassador to
Spain, but that sinecure was given to a mestizo much closer to
the Leader and his wife than I. It was also a reward; the ambassador and his wife had been the guardians of the Leader's
illegitimate daughter by Mimi Cardenas, his mistress. I had assisted him in his ruthless climb to power, having fully understood the compulsions that drove the man. I did not go to him
to ask for that posting—I got to him through the mistress he
could not deny.

I had known Mimi since she was in college, as she had

worked briefly for me as a secretary. She came from an impoverished Ermita family, mestizo, of course. She had starred in college plays, could sing a little, and that was how she attracted me and, after me, the Leader. Their liaison was blessed with this daughter, now in school in Switzerland. It was Mimi who told me the Leader and his wife were planning a state visit to Latin America, that an embassy in Peru was to be opened.

As I said, I would have preferred the embassy in Spain. And why not? I had salted away much of my wealth—The Yolk!— in the mother country. I had houses in Madrid, Barcelona and San Sebastian; properties in Andalucia; housing estates in Majorca; banks in Bilbao, Sevilla and Madrid. And I donated a magnificent museum for Spanish contemporary art in Alicante. Didn't my father and all those Spanish priests in Manila support Franco and his Falangists?

And so it happened. I was in Madrid in 1973 when the Leader himself called. Mimi had really gone to work on my behalf. The Leader said I should return to Manila immediately and get ready to leave for Peru.

Now, let me make this clear, for there are those naive spirits who think it was easy to say no to the Leader. The consequences of denying him may not be immediately forthcoming, but they will surely come, for the man had a retentive memory. There were, to be sure, snide objections to my ambassadorship—these I learned later from the ministry people who recorded these diligently, that I would use the post for my own purposes. But what government official hasn't done this? My loyalties were dubious, but in those times, loyalty to the Leader was loyalty to the nation. It was that simple.

I hurried to the palace and the Leader was pleased that I had accepted. What were the policies he wanted me to pursue in Peru? "As your personal emissary, your goodwill is my first responsibility. But, Mr. President, I need to be briefed on the details."

He smiled benignly. "That is what I like about you, Carling.

But you really don't need instructions. You speak excellent Spanish, you are cultured, urbane—and rich! The government support is small. Budgetary restrictions . . ."

I immediately understood; I was expected to donate my money.

I asked for the dossiers of the people who were to accompany me, particularly those who could speak Spanish, who also had some knowledge of South America. I had a long talk with my deputy, a career officer, and told him he would have the run of the embassy. At the same time, I made it clear to him that he would hang if he bungled, but would be rewarded magnificently by Cobello y Cia if I triumphed. I brought two of my own men to backstop him, paid by Cobello y Cia, five of my Sta. Mesa household staff and my favorite niece as my private secretary.

The embassy in Lima was an old gray building, the residence in similar antiquated condition. I had both refurbished with new drapes, carpets, furniture, plumbing, electric fixtures. My staff—I did something that endeared me to them and also polished my democratic image. I took them one by one to lunch or dinner at the Club Excelsior, Lima's snootiest social club, of which I had immediately become a member. They told me later that no ambassador had ever invited the lowliest janitor or driver to dine with him.

I can see myself again, resplendent in my jusi barong and tuxedo trousers, at the glittering receptions in Pizarro Palace. I can hear my voice, the cadence and poetry of Spanish as only urbane and cultured men can express themselves. How I loved Lima, felt at home not so much with the history impregnated in this venerable capital but because I shared with the mestizo aristocracy its affinity with Spain—none of the embedded cravings for indigenous culture, the loathing of priests prevalent in Mexico and the often anti-Spanish sentiments as the bedrock of Filipino nationalism. The elite in Peru is white and I easily fitted in it, surrounded now by people of similar racial and social inclinations.

But Delfin—my son! My son! He would have no appreciation of such lofty sentiments. He is much too involved with the rabble, the lazy, stinking Indios, and it is they who will inherit the earth! *Qué barbaridad!*

13

Let me backtrack a little again. One morning, in mid-May in 1963, Cornejo at the gate came to me. Angela, about six years old then, Corito and I were having breakfast on the terrace, which, the day before, had been washed by rain. The potted bromeliads shone and portions of the marble were still glazed with water. Cornejo had been with us for more than a decade, his father before him also our gatekeeper. He kept the gate closed at all times, opening the side door only to the servants and to guests who were properly announced or were expected. Like most of the help, he was from the hacienda, dark of skin, with a diffident smile that was a kind of mask. It was with this meaningless smile that he approached us. I was having my favorite fried rice with garlic, sliced tomatoes with salted eggs and strong Batangas coffee.

"Señorito, a young man at the gate wants to see you. He came yesterday afternoon. He is a *provinciano,* tall, about seventeen or eighteen years old. I told him I cannot let him in and he said he will not leave until he has seen you. All he has with him is a small canvas bag. When I looked outside this morning, he was asleep by the gate. It is good it did not rain last night else he would have been very wet."

"What does he want?" My interest was aroused.

"He said he does not want anything, just to see you and talk with you. Not more than ten minutes, he said. I examined his bag—just a few old clothes. I searched him. No weapons. Not even a small knife . . ."

"Let him in," I said.

I will never forget the first time I saw Delfin. I was through with breakfast and was just sipping my coffee. Corito and Angela were finished, too, but had stayed on at the table, curious about this insistent visitor.

Delfin walked into our presence with what seemed like cocksure confidence and as he stood before me, he bowed slightly and said "Good morning, sir" crisply in well-pronounced English. He glanced at Angela and Corito and nodded toward them in greeting, too.

There he stood and a shock of recognition quickly coursed through me; he looked exactly like me in my youth though a little bit darker—the same wide brow, the straight nose and that chin. He was poorly dressed in faded khaki pants and white shirt, but there was about him an unmistakable look of aristocracy.

"What do you want to see me for?"

He glanced again at Angela and Corito. "May I speak alone with you, sir?"

"This is my sister and my niece," I said. "You may speak in their presence."

He stood stiffly, head bowed a little. When he refused to speak, I knew then that he meant what he said. I stood up and he followed me to the library, his eyes wandering over those shelves and shelves of books. I had added quite a lot to them in the recent past, particularly the antiquarian editions that were presented to me by dealers.

I sat at one end of the long narra reading table and asked him to sit beside me, but he merely stood, thanking me first. Then, with just the two of us, he finally spoke, softly, as if he did not want anyone else to hear.

"Severina—my mother—died last December. I had asked her so many times in the past who my father was, but she never told me. I stopped asking her after a while. Then, before she died, she told me . . ." He paused.

Every word sank into me, boulders in a quagmire of reverie, and a hundred immobilized memories long dispersed into the void came back alive and whole again, swamping me, drowning me.

He continued evenly, "She asked me to see you, that I must promise her I would. And now that I have seen you and have fulfilled my promise to my mother, I must go." And with that final word, he turned and marched out of the room.

I sat there, paralyzed by emotions I could not explain or control; the revelation confirmed me, buoyed me. *I have a son, a handsome grown-up son!* Dr. Avecilla had examined my sperm count after the dread disease was vanquished and he said I would never be able to sire a child; that was one ravage of the disease that could not be reversed. I was therefore confident in all my liaisons, the women I had with just a finger on the telephone, the cloying attention of my cousins' lovely daughters. I need not be responsible. But I had a son! A son, and the whole world that wonderful morning changed completely. In a while, however, I realized that the boy had walked out of my life. I rushed out of the house in my plaid silk robe and asked a bewildered Cornejo at the gate where the boy had gone. He pointed toward the main highway; in my bedroom slippers I ran in that direction, to the mélange of buses and jeepneys jostling one another to the city.

I saw him with his canvas bag about to board a jeepney. I rushed after him and held on to the handle of the jeepney as it started. I was dragged along before I pitched myself into the jeepney—fortunately, there was a seat beside him. I held his arm, "I must talk with you, *hijo*. You cannot leave me like this." I realized I was pleading.

The driver stopped the jeepney.

The boy must have been embarrassed by the attention I had drawn, my attire and all, so he followed me down out of the jeepney. Walking beside him back to the house, this pride, this vaulting sense of being a father, this great paternal feeling I had never felt before filled me, never, not even for Angela, although I loved her so much; maybe because she was a girl and was always there when I needed her.

We were now in the shade of the huge acacia trees along this street that led to the house. I would have ridden the jeepney to wherever it was going had he not agreed to get off. I think he realized this, too. It would have been my first jeepney ride, for even in the days after the war when there was very limited transportation, my family always had our own—jeeps and command carriers, which Father got from the American army. And, soon after, our first Buick and Cadillac arrived.

I asked Delfin where he was going and he said it was to a distant aunt somewhere in Parañaque. He had arrived the day before and from the pier he had gone straight to the house. Did he have money? It was a foolish question, but I wanted to know. Yes, he said with some pride, what Severina had saved, all three hundred pesos of it, pinned inside his shirt so no pickpocket could reach it.

At the gate, I instructed a flustered gatekeeper to let Delfin in at any time he wished. It was Sunday and though I worked even on Sundays, this time I decided to stay in the house and be with him.

How does one become an instant father? All my life I have

had my way. With money, I got anything I wanted; almost anything anyway. Could I now buy this young man's affection? He had had no supper the previous evening, no breakfast, this I soon realized. I took him back to the dining room and told the cook to prepare breakfast, and for me another cup of coffee.

So many questions ached to be asked, but I held back, and watched him eat silently. When I did ask, he spoke slowly, as if he were weighing every uttered word.

To my pleasure, he said he was enrolling at the state university. He had a full scholarship through the efforts of the high school principal who recognized, perhaps, the boy's academic excellence. He was his high school's valedictorian that year. I knew little of the island where Severina had gone—that Siquijor was somewhere in the Visayas, minuscule, insignificant, without any industry. I would ask my office the following morning to prepare its profile.

And what did he want to be? What course in the university would he be taking?

Not one hesitant moment. "I hope I can be a lawyer, sir," he said simply. Almost immediately, I knew that he would achieve that goal.

I had presumed that I could persuade him to stay. How many rooms in the house were empty? How many servants did we have to serve just the three of us? Maybe I sounded too eager when I said, "*Hijo,* live with me. There is so much space here—there is just my sister and her daughter and I . . ."

Again, no hesitation. "Thank you very much, sir. All that I promised my mother was to see you."

At this moment my precious Angela came to the dining room and sat beside me to look at Delfin. She had heard part of the conversation.

"Your cousin," I said, almost blurting out "your sister" instead. Though in poor health, Angela would surely grow into a beauty—the signs were explicit, the large dark eyes, the angelic face—indeed, her name truly fitted her and her disposition as well.

Delfin and I were talking in English. His Tagalog was not any better than mine and it was heavily accented.

"Tito." Angela had been calling me uncle since she could speak. Her hand was on mine, but those limpid eyes were on the young man before us. "Why does he not want to stay with us? Then you don't have to help me with my homework. I can ask him to do that."

I told her in Spanish that this young man was my son, that I really wanted him to stay, and when I turned to Delfin, something in his face told me he understood everything. I was to learn later that, indeed, he knew enough Spanish to get by—Severina had taught him what she had learned in the house. It was only a matter of time, in college and by his own reading, that he would know Spanish, speak it correctly in a manner better than mine.

Perhaps I tried too hard. I could imagine his uneasiness not just with me but with the grand dimensions of the house. He need not tell me how he had lived and grown up in that godforsaken island. The roughness of his skin, his big callused hands were more than eloquent expressions of how harshly he had lived.

But why did Severina never tell me that we had a child? Why did she leave without telling me? Later on, it would have been easy for her to write. I could only surmise that it was my parents' doing. How often had they dinned into me that I must never marry someone whose social background was inadequate.

Having finished breakfast, he stood up, bowed and thanked me. "I must go now, sir," he said.

I couldn't hold him back, so I decided to take him to his aunt. I would at least know in what anonymous corner of Parañaque he would stay.

Angela wanted to come along. She sat between Delfin and me. The Cadillac, the fifth in the garage, was new, black and shiny. A couple of Mercedes-Benzes were awaiting release at the piers.

Delfin gave the address to the driver with some hesitation. All the way to Parañaque, he did not speak unless he was spoken to. Angela asked her own kind of questions: Did he live by the sea in this Siquijor island? No, but the sea was not far. Did he do a lot of swimming and boating? Angela loved the sea and when I would take the boat from the yacht club for a breath of sea air along the Bataan or Cavite coasts, she always wanted to come along. Yes, Delfin told her—he also liked swimming and fishing.

It took us more than an hour to locate the place, tucked inside a narrow alley into which the Cadillac could not squeeze. We walked through a seedy neighborhood, ramshackle wooden houses. It was Angela's first time in a slum; her face was so mobile that, although she did not speak, the shock was all over her young face. The whole place smelled, too, of abandoned urinals and dour living, and this is where my son was going to live.

I met the distant aunt, a fat, slovenly woman, middle-aged and worldly-wise, who immediately recognized my social status. She could glimpse through the narrow alley the El Dorado parked on the street around which the children and the neighborhood riffraff were now crowded. Her manner was sickeningly ingratiating, saying how fortunate that Delfin had such well-to-do relatives and, now, he had to visit such a humble place blessed though he was with the acquaintanceship of such generous people.

She had opened the door of the tiny apartment; some slattern women were inside, squatting on the cement floor, smoking and playing cards. Delfin walked me back to the car and, before we parted, I thrust into his pocket a fistful of bills. He did not want to accept it.

"I will come back for you," I said, dodging his hand as he tried to shove the money at me.

Angela went into the car immediately as if she were anxious to be inside, to be shielded from the destitution and squalor she had just seen. She seemed very relieved when we finally left.

"He is going to stay there?" she asked in disbelief.

In the office the following morning I sent an aide to the state university to inquire about Delfin's scholarship, specifically how much it was worth, for how long. What about his textbooks? The other expenses he might incur? I wanted to know all about his needs.

The aide returned. Delfin had a full scholarship, which meant he also had a little spending money, but he had to maintain his high grades to retain the stipend and the scholarship. With so many other bright young people at the university on scholarships, he might have some difficulty keeping his. How could he concentrate on his studies while living in that dreadful place? The stipend was measly—would it keep him alive? I was very glad when at the opening of the school year, he transferred to a tiny room near the campus. His having to commute to Parañaque every day was a terrible waste of time.

✖

The profile prepared by my research department was comprehensive. None of my ships stopped in Dumaguete, the port closest to the island. Three hours by ferry from Siquijor and you are in Dumaguete and, from there, connections by air or boat to any of the country's big cities.

Though densely populated, the island is basically agricultural, with almost no potential for industry. For tourism, it has white sand beaches and snorkeling possibilities in its coral reefs, many of them teeming with fish, particularly skipjacks and the rare blue ribbon eel.

A coastal road, some seventy-six kilometers long, skirts the island and all its towns. It is hilly, limestone-ridged. The natives are fishermen, and farmers tending coconut, corn, cassava, abaca, rice, peanuts and tobacco. Some manganese is mined in the interior.

What attracted me most, however, were the details about the island's history and its identification with the black arts.

The islanders' oral tradition holds that Siquijor rose from the sea amid thunder and lightning, and also describes a legendary King Kihod. Fossilized sea creatures have been found in the interior highlands. Chinese porcelain plowed up by local farmers indicates the prevalence of pre-Hispanic trading. The island's native name was Katugasan, after *tugas*— the molave trees that covered the hills. The Spanish first called it Isla del Fuego (Island of Fire), probably due to the swarms of fireflies they found here, and later renamed it Siquijor.

In spite of the long presence of Christianity, Siquijor is noted for herbal medicine, witchcraft, magic and superstition, with San Antonio as the center of shamanism. There are said to be about fifty *mananambals* who are classified as either "white" or "black" sorcerers, depending on whether they specialize in healing or harming. You can see a collection of their paraphernalia, including voodoo dolls, potions and concoctions, skulls and candles at Silliman University's Anthropology Museum in Dumaguete. San Antonio, named after the patron saint of medicine, is reached by a back road leading into the interior hills, but don't expect to see much evidence of the dark arts.

During Holy Week, herbalists and sorcerers come from all over the Visayas and Mindanao to San Antonio to participate in a ritual known as *tang-alap*. They roam the area's forests, caves and cemeteries to gather medicinal herbs and roots, then sit in a circle, and while a humorous mood prevails, the ingredients are combined in piles. The gathering culminates in an exclusive ritual that takes place in a secluded cave at dawn.

Magbabarang is the name given to the "black" sorcerers. These dreaded purveyors of pain and death can be hired as agents of vengeance, and use *barang*—certain bees, beetles and centipedes that have an extra leg—and magic invocations to achieve their ends. They collect these insects and keep them in a bamboo tube. Always on a Friday, they place several pieces of paper, each bearing someone's name and address, in the tube. They check a short time later, and if the papers have been shredded, it's taken as a sign that the insects will attack the individuals named. The *magbabarang* ties a white string around the insects' other legs before releasing them. They are ordered to find their victims, enter their bodies and cause death by biting the internal organs. Then they return to their master, who examines the strings to see if the magic was successful. If so, the string will be red with blood; if it's clean, it means the person was innocent and could resist the hex. Those who suspect that a *magbabarang* had been hired against them may employ their own practitioner to counteract the voodoo, which could result in a complex power struggle.

Later that year, during Holy Week, an aide came in excitedly. He had helped prepare the Siquijor profile. Now, he showed me an Agence France Presse dispatch:

"WITCHES" CONVERGE ON SIQUIJOR ISLAND
TO TEST POTENCY OF THEIR MEDICINES

Self-styled medicine men, sorcerers, herbalists and other practitioners of esoteric arts converged on this Visayan island this Holy Week to cook up their most potent potions.

Such medicine men could be seen in the island's cemeteries on Good Friday, picking up gravel with their hands from the base of the graves for use in their potions.

The annual event has earned Siquijor the title of "the island of witches."

It has also given its inhabitants a fearsome reputation among fellow Filipinos—much to the irritation of some of Siquijor's more image-conscious residents.

From Good Friday until Easter, various people described

alternately as healers, witches, shamans and medicine men prepared the various mixes that they will use all year.

Ingredients for potions were gathered on Friday, cooked in cauldrons on Saturday and made into various preparations that the sorcerers sell.

Most ingredients are from Siquijor's forests: plants, leaves, twigs, vines and roots. Some "treatments" from these materials seem to be much like traditional herbal medicine since they supposedly alleviate aches, pains and various diseases.

Only plants from Siquijor will do, although some herbalists readily admit these plants grow elsewhere.

But some potions use even stranger ingredients: cemetery dirt and wood gathered on Good Friday, and leftover candlewax and flower petals scavenged from Holy Week processions.

Florian Cabico, a 68-year-old herbalist from the nearby island of Cebu who travels to Siquijor each year, says the potions must be prepared on Good Friday because "there is no God on Good Friday."

This refers to the belief among Catholics that Good Friday marks the death of Christ, who is not resurrected until Easter Sunday. The Philippines is largely Roman Catholic, but animist beliefs persist in many areas of everyday life.

Medicine men say their potions have supernatural effects: charms that allow the wearers to dodge bullets, prevent them from falling off coconut trees, and ensure good luck.

There are charms that guarantee salesmen big earnings, preparations that draw fish into nets and love potions for both men and women.

But the most feared are the curses: spells cast by witches using voodoolike dolls and, through offerings of food and drink, to unseen spirits in a hidden ceremony within the gnarled roots of the "balete" tree, widely believed by Filipinos to be an abode of unearthly creatures.

Such witches, both male and female, can supposedly bring illnesses and even painful death to their enemies—or anyone they are paid to curse. Fortunately, sorcerers also prepare charms to counter these.

Medicine men, who often live as simple farmers alongside the rest of the communities in rural towns here, will rarely admit they are also witches who cast curses, due to possible retaliation from their victims' relatives.

But people in their neighborhood will say—out of earshot—who among them practice such black arts.

Other Siquijor medicine men reputedly have even stranger skills, like the ability to walk on hot coals or charm snakes by reciting certain prayers or, in one case, to make spirits animate paper dolls so they dance to disco music.

Many medicine men insist they are good Catholics who see no conflict between their practices and their faith.

Juan Ponce, 70, describes himself as a Catholic and says he uses his potions only to "cure sicknesses that can't be cured in hospitals."

Ponce, considered a teacher by a small clique of younger herbalists who gather at his home from throughout the country each year, says his knowledge was passed on to him from his father, who received it from his own father.

I know, of course, that witchcraft, a heritage of ghosts and the macabre, is not confined to Siquijor. Every village has its lore of the mysterious, a past beyond fathoming, enshrined in myth for the young to embellish and perhaps to believe in— the trees that are the abode of spirits, the turn of a river where a nymph was once seen, an empty lot where on moonlit nights wraiths in white reveled.

✠

One Sunday morning, having fulfilled my duty to Corito for the day, we fell to talking about Delfin.

"I find him very attractive," Corito said. She had gotten dressed but was still lounging on my bed. "You know who he reminds me of? You—when there was more stamina here," she said, fingering my crotch.

"He is barely out of his teens," I said.

"That's when they are the most sturdy, too," she said. "And you know, he looks just like you, darker eyes, but so very handsome . . ."

I knew exactly what she was saying. "Now, Corito," I said

rather testily, "whatever is in your mind, just keep it there. He is my son, your nephew—don't you forget that!"

She rose and started laughing, her laughter in sonorous volleys of joyless mirth. She turned around, looked at me and said clearly, "Your son, my nephew—and you, Carling—you are my brother!" and turning abruptly, she left me to ponder the irony and the truth of what she had uttered.

I now realized how truly I wanted Delfin. In those times when I socialized and the talk veered to family and children, I had kept silent. As I said, I wanted my private life unintruded upon, even in conversation. I was now delighted to talk openly, fondly even, of my son, raising as I did curiosity and skepticism, that I was perhaps joking, or enlivening a particularly asinine conversation.

I'll let you in on a little secret, I would say with a conspiratorial smile. I did get married long ago, but she died.

And when they pressed for details, I would clam up. But where was this Delfin, this brilliant boy who had my name, my looks?

You will see, I told them proudly. You will see.

And then I would announce boastfully, He is a scholar at the state university. You can always check the veracity of this statement. He is a Cobello. His first name is Delfin.

Having revealed those details, I saw more than ever how important it was that he move to Sta. Mesa. He never called or visited, however. Always, it was I who went to see him, and I had to suffer my pride, which I never did in the past. I was capable of noblesse oblige, particularly with those in my employ who had served me and my family for so long, but with people who were seemingly equal, to them I showed no mercy. At forty, I think I had gotten the reputation in business of being astute—and ruthless—and I nurtured that image so that anyone with intentions of crossing my path would be forewarned, would then beware. And rarely did anyone taunt me.

It was difficult for me to understand why a boy who had obviously lived in want in some dilapidated village in the Visayas would reject the ease and comfort that I offered, circumstances that were legitimately his and were all being gladly given. If I were he, I would have grabbed everything.

How did Severina raise him? To loathe me perhaps for having abandoned her? But I did not know. Why then did she bother at all at the last moment to reveal my identity? Thinking back, I realized how culpable I was. When she left, I should have inquired about her whereabouts from the help. I should have persevered, threatened them even, particularly her distant aunt, the cook. If I had persevered, I am sure they would have told me. I could then have found her and her baby. But would I have stood by her? Again, the warning from my parents, their wish to keep our property intact, to see that our bloodline, the Spanish in it, was strengthened, not diluted. And to the wealth that Corito and I inherited, I had already added so much on my own. What was one house for Delfin in Diliman? I could build it with a snap of a finger. I kept several houses. And I seldom visited them, nor did Corito and Angela, for now Corito always wanted to be where I was, wanted me beside her when she needed me, always using Angela as bait, as an excuse, that the girl was not well again. And, God, most of the time it was true. But though I wanted to build Delfin a house, I could not do it without his consent.

Without his being aware, I knew not only about the tiny room he kept but also his schedule in school. I tried not to be conspicuous in my attention. I knew he resented my wish to pamper him.

✠

The driver had carefully timed it; Delfin would be coming out of the Liberal Arts building at noon, his Friday afternoons being free, and the car drove over to the sidewalk. I had gotten out of the car and there was no way he could avoid me. "I want to invite you to lunch, *hijo*," I said.

He turned briefly to a couple of classmates who were with him; they were staring at me, at the Cadillac with a uniformed driver. It was the first time in four months that I had seen him, but an aide had kept tabs, every month handing him an envelope with cash that would enable him to be comfortable. He had at first refused it, but the aide had pleaded with him that I would fire him if he did not do his job. That was quick thinking but, in truth, I never told him that.

Delfin smiled at me, warmly enough, I think. He wore the same faded khaki pants, white shirt and battered sneakers. He had also lost a bit of that sun-browned skin and he was fairer now. I saw myself in him again, only he was taller, though not by much.

"Thank you, sir, but I have plans this afternoon."

I held his arm firmly and led him to the Cadillac. "Tell me about it in the car," I said. I was prepared to drag him and I think he sensed that.

He was tight-lipped and glum, speaking only when I spoke to him. It occurred to me to be blunt. "Delfin, what ugly things did your mother tell you about me?"

The question must have startled him. He looked at me in surprise. "You never knew my mother, sir. She was a good person, with never an unkind word for anyone. She never spoke about you till, like I said, she was already very ill. And all that she said was that I should see you, that you should know."

I was mortified. "We are going to the Polo Club," I said. Then I called Corito on the car radio; she was at the Assumption waiting for Angela. Both would proceed to the Club from school.

Makati was growing magnificently, an enclave of business, banking, its residential areas well planned for the rich. My own office building was already almost finished, thirty stories tall. I was also going to build a house in Dasmariñas. It would be more convenient to entertain there. I wanted a place to stay where I was not always at Corito's side. The Huk rebellion was over, its members having turned into mere brigands. It had bothered me and Father, too, but we knew Magsaysay, who was then president, would defeat them and come to the succor of the oligarchy.

My businesses were thriving, too, but it seemed I had learned so little about empathy. I could not understand Delfin's deep longing for independence, his desire to challenge the world and live on his wits and brawn in a manner I never fostered in my own self, used as I was to the privileges of birth and high station. Where did all that granite perseverance come from? From Severina and her peasant origins? I was beginning to appreciate my son as someone different from me. I would never be able to do what he was now doing.

The drive along Highway 54, soon to be known as EDSA, was quiet but tense. Corito and Angela were already at the Club. The two often came here on weekends to ride, Corito to shed off some pounds, and Angela to exercise. At eight, she was tall but oh so thin. They were on the patio drinking Coke. Always, Delfin was polite as he greeted them. He remained standing until I told him to sit down. Angela never stopped gazing at him, smiling. On the sunny polo field, the stable boys were walking some of the horses. A waiter came and took our orders.

It was a leisurely lunch, chopped endives with oil and vinegar, chateaubriand and Spanish sherry. Angela had very little appetite; I had to finish her steak. She was very much alive, however, not quiet and seemingly lost. She had a lot of questions like "I would like to visit you. Will you take me to your place one day?"

Delfin merely smiled at her.

"Tito said you have moved from that place where we first

took you. I am very glad you did. But you can live in Sta. Mesa—I cannot understand why you don't want to. We have so many empty rooms." She turned to her mother. "That room next to mine, there's nothing there but cabinets and cabinets. Sometimes, at night, I think there is a ghost there—no, you don't want that room. But the room across the hall?"

Corito would do anything to please her daughter. "You must come," she said graciously, warmly. "Why don't you visit? The weekends when you don't have classes. Help Angela with her homework . . ."

Again, a noncommittal smile. I was very happy that Corito and Angela had voiced my feelings without my prodding. Corito knew who he was, she had seen Severina and me in an embrace, but she did not show any sign of jealousy anymore—and anyhow, Severina was dead. The whole house knew Delfin was my son and there, in the Club, I wished there were people now who knew me, who would approach our table.

Angela couldn't be stopped. "Why don't you want to come even if we want you so much? What is the reason, Delf?" she had given Delfin a nickname.

"I would like to very much," he finally said. "But I want to be on my own, to learn how to be independent."

An honest answer, and I was grateful for it.

Just as I had hoped, Don Simeon, who owned the Agricultural and Industrial Bank where I had a minority interest, happened by. He knew Corito and Angela. I stood up and introduced Delfin, who had also risen. "My son, Simeon."

The banker stepped back, looked Delfin over, then grinned and pumped my son's hand. "So it is true—what I heard about you having a son. But you know, Charlie, he is handsomer than you and, I hope, brighter, too, although that would take a lot of doing."

We laughed. Delfin was blushing. Don Simeon was twenty years older than I, mestizo, too, and to Delfin he said, "I presume you are still in school, *hijo*. What are you going to be?"

He hesitated, and I answered for him. "He is a scholar at the state university. He is studying law."

Don Simeon chuckled. "So he will replace Jake when he is through, huh?"

"If Delfin so chooses," I said, suavely, considering his feelings.

Don Simeon was looking for a table. I asked him to join us so he would be able to know Delfin better. That is how business relationships start, from social beginnings. I wanted, in fact, to introduce Delfin to as many of my associates and connections as possible, if only he deigned stay with us. But Don Simeon was expecting company and it was enough that he had met Delfin. Everyone would soon know the reality of my son—and heir.

14

When Delfin said he had plans that afternoon, I suspected he had quickly concocted a reason for staying away, for it was Friday and I had hoped he would be able to be with me not just that afternoon but perhaps for the weekend. I did not want to appear as if I were begging. Angela was now having her favorite *macapuno*—coconut—ice cream and Corito always appreciated the cheesecake. It was almost three in the afternoon. I took Delfin to Francesco, my Italian tailor for the last five years, and, there, Delfin was fitted for a couple of summer suits and one for fall. I also ordered for him several shirts and summer trousers. I told him I would like to take him on one of my trips and, please, give away that old pair of khakis and get several pairs of new shoes. As a haberdasher, Francesco also had a good line of Italian shoes for men.

Delfin did not object to Francesco; he stood there, acceding to the master cutter's measuring him, and all the while Francesco was saying how splendid he looked, what a handsome mannequin he would make at a fashion show. Francesco was homosexual.

It was one of the most pleasant afternoons I had ever spent with Delfin. We hadn't talked at length before and I wanted so much to know about him, his boyhood, his needs.

"I am doing all right, sir," he said. "I am earning a little . . ."

And what could a prelaw scholar, studying rigorously to maintain his scholarship, do to earn money?

He was candid; he said he helped some of his classmates with their reports and he also tutored a couple of girls from nearby Maryknoll in math—he was good at it and had considered taking up a science degree, but had decided on law instead.

Was it his ambition to be a politician? We were in the car on our way to my office. I wanted my senior staff to see him.

"No, sir, that's farthest from my mind."

"Stop calling me 'sir,' " I said, a little peeved. "Call me Papa, *hijo,* if you can manage it."

He did not reply. I knew then he would never call me Papa, and the old hurt came back, the suspicion that Severina must have coached him, pounded into his young mind that I had done them wrong.

"You did not explain to me why you want to be a lawyer."

This time, he hesitated and, then, again the truth: "In Siquijor, sir, there are many people who are made even poorer because they have no way of fighting back, because they cannot afford lawyers . . ." and as if he was suddenly aware of having said too much, he stopped.

Was this my son talking about championing the poor? Youthful idealism, I concluded; I had heard a bit of that from some of my classmates at the Ateneo, like Jake, my chief counsel, for instance, but they soon forget it all when they enter the real world, the world which I dominate.

My Makati building was ready, and the finishing touches were being completed in the upper floors. My office was on the ground floor, unlike other executives who want their offices higher up. My penthouse, however, was there at the top, where I had a view of the city. It was accessible only to me, with its private elevator.

All my top people were also on the ground floor. We did not go to my office through my rear entrance but through the front so that as we walked through executive country, all of them could see Delfin. I did not have to introduce him—by his looks alone they could see he was the son I had been boasting about.

In my office, I told him to sit down and read *The Wall Street Journal* and the *Financial Times* while I sifted through the messages that had come in during the late morning and lunch hour. Tina, my private secretary, came in with her pad and more messages. She was older than I; I had inherited her from Father. She was fat, jovial and extremely efficient. We always spoke in Spanish, and I introduced Delfin to her. "I have heard a lot about you," she said in Spanish, presuming Delfin spoke Spanish, too. "You are so handsome and you look just like your father."

Delfin smiled and replied in English, "Thank you, ma'am, for the compliment."

Nothing of importance from Tina or in the papers on my desk. I took him to the rear, to the private elevator and to the top, my penthouse. I often stayed here when I had company or when I entertained a maximum of eight people. For more, I used the house in Dasmariñas. Going now to Sta. Mesa was too much of a bother—the distance, the knotted traffic and the pollution that seeped through the air-conditioning. My building was taller than almost all the other Makati buildings and, from the penthouse, Manila sprawled in all directions. Were it not for the acacia trees, I could see the house in Sta. Mesa. On one side was the helicopter pad and the anchored helicopter, kept in readiness if I wanted to go to the beach house in

Bataan, or to the hacienda, or even to Sta. Mesa if I was in a hurry. I had not meant to show all these possessions or even my lifestyle to Delfin. I had wanted privacy with him, to know him and, looking back, I suppose I had awed him somewhat, for now he was rigidly silent.

But even if I did not show him all these, maybe, bright as he was, he already knew the extent of my holdings.

"I sometimes stay here, *hijo*," I said. I took him to the other bedroom. And then I made the pitch. "If you will be uneasy staying in Sta. Mesa, you can stay here with me. I will not bother you—in any case, I am not here often. As you know, I am often away on business trips, or I am in Sta. Mesa, or in that other house in Dasmariñas . . ."

When he did not reply, I knew I was again rejected.

What could I possibly do to gain my own son's affection?

Here I am, one of the country's richest, most powerful men, but with him, I am completely powerless.

My own son! I survey the supreme magnitude of my economic achievement and a chest-thumping sense of pride buoys me. I had really used Corito's and my own inheritance to grow, to parlay all these into something my father had never dreamed of. Like him, I had gotten to meet the important people in government and out. I had helped them, too, contributed not just to their political agenda but also to their own pockets, and they had all responded—the reparations, the lumber concessions, the licenses and franchises and the approval of Congress—even my income tax deductions. I had a battery of brilliant people, most of them lawyers, who knew all the loopholes, and some of them even proclaimed themselves as nationalists—I lured them, paid them homage, co-opted them, then used them all.

And why shouldn't they believe in me? I was collecting Philippine antiques, Chinese porcelain, preserving them, even created an exhibition hall for my collection in the absence of a national museum. I gave away prizes in literature, supported the local stage and charity! All this, recorded dutifully by journalists, is nationalism indeed.

What will I talk about with Delfin, my reading, my knowledge of Roman law, the lines I could remember from the Roman orators? Yeats and T. S. Eliot—do not forget, my dear reader, that I had dabbled in poetry, that I love poetry, thanks to those many idle days during the Occupation in the brothel in Pasay when I was always reading. But would showing off my intellect bring me closer to my son? I doubted it—he might even conclude that I was just showing off, for that is what I did at board meetings when my ignoramus colleagues would ask me who it was this time I was quoting and, sometimes, although it was my very own thoughts, I would attribute them to some Chinese or Indian philosopher—nonexistent, of course, but who among them would know? *Cobello locuta est, causa finita est!* (Cobello has spoken, the dispute is finished!)

Then, it occurred to me. I would take Delfin to Nueva Ecija, to Hacienda Esperanza—he would certainly like to see where his mother came from, maybe even to meet some of his mother's relatives who were still there.

"I will take you to Nueva Ecija this afternoon. Cancel all your plans. I have not been there myself in a long time . . ."

I could see at once the pleasure light his face. "Yes, sir," he said. "Thank you."

My impulse had worked. Finally, I was going to do something he approved of.

The house in San Quentin had always been maintained so that if I ever decided to visit the place, I would be comfortable. I called Sta. Mesa and told the cook to prepare to leave for San Quentin; Corito and Angela had just come in, too, and Corito said she would take Angela with her. It would be a wonderful weekend for the family.

Delfin said he had brought no clothes, so I flung open one

of the cabinets. "Take anything you want," I said. "I am sure they will fit you, taller though you are, but not by much." He was embarrassed, hesitant. I picked a suitcase and started filling it.

I am not a finicky dresser. In the last three years, Francesco had made me only four dozen suits, but he likes to announce that he is my tailor. I have, at most, only a dozen tuxedos and another dozen old tweed jackets, mostly Donegals. When my three-button gray flannel suits tailored in the fifties went out of fashion in the seventies, I still wore them because all were of fine English wool. In fact, I sometimes wear a five-dollar tie picked up on a New York sidewalk with my Savile Row suits because I like the traditional Brooks Brothers design. All these may seem excessive until one realizes I have several houses abroad and in each there are enough clothes for any season. My only one caprice is white silk shirts, all made to order in Hong Kong with a red monogram above the breast pocket: C.C.

I had to go back to my office to sign some papers. Delfin sat there, reading the newspapers and business magazines. He sauntered over to the shelves that line one side of my office— more Philippine books there, some rare editions, some sociology classics, fiction, history. He browsed until I was through and my secretary had also received instructions in the event that important matters cropped up that weekend.

15

We arrived in San Quentin shortly after eight P.M. The house was ablaze with lights. The generator in the back was humming and would continue to do so the whole night. Angela met us at the landing and she kissed me and stood on tiptoe to kiss Delfin as well. It was the first time, I think, that she kissed him.

Anselmo, the *encargado* for that part of the hacienda planted to rice, was at the landing, ever ready to jump at my bidding. He was fair of skin, maybe of Spanish or Chinese ancestry. His father had been *encargado*, and Anselmo's oldest son would probably get the job, too.

I had not visited the hacienda for more than a year and had entrusted so much to this man. I had used it as collateral in many transactions and it had served us well. I have always tried to be one step—no, three steps—ahead in my thinking about traditional agriculture and saw the opportunities in manufacturing, food processing and other industries that are agriculture-based. From there, I had hoped that with technology transferred from the United States or Japan, I could expand into light industry.

The house is on the eastern edge of the town, at the end of a long road lined, as in Sta. Mesa, with acacia trees that my grandfather had planted. It is not on the main road, but it cannot be missed because it is the biggest house in San Quentin, larger than the *municipio,* with its wide lot and stable for horses in the back, although the stable had not been in use for many years because seldom did Corito and I go horseback riding in the hacienda like we used to when we were children. The house is roofed with tile, so old that grass had sprouted in the cracks; the walls are brick, plastered over. Two of the upstairs bedrooms had lowered ceilings to make them easier to air-condition. The staff at the house really did nothing except clean it, and because they never knew when we would come, it was always neat and the floors shiny. Now they were lined up at the landing, too, eager smiles plastered on their faces. They know that when we leave, all of them will be given additional money. All of them, too, would have better fare, for when the cook came she always brought along more food than we could consume.

Behind the house is the water tower, a steel cylindrical tank painted red, perched on iron girders as tall as a buri palm. As a boy, I would climb the tower, usually late in the afternoon, and sit on the shelf below the tank and watch the sun sink in a blaze of reds and purples at the rim of the world—the ripening grain a shining golden ocean in October. In July, that same landscape would become water-logged fields, a vast crisscrossed mirror awaiting the transplanting of rice seedlings. Beyond the rice fields, in the far distance, is the rimless expanse of green— the cane fields stretching as far as the eye can see and, in the horizon, the twin smokestacks of the Cobello sugar mill, a wisp of smoke curling above it. And, across the graying sky, a white blur of herons swooping down for their evening meal of tadpoles. Beholding this glorious plain, I would be filled with that exhilarating sense of possession, of pride, knowing all this would be mine.

Now the rice fields are fallow and brown and the emerald vastness of growing rice is yet to come and, after that, the sweet fragrance of ripening grain and newly cut hay would swirl all around and drift into the big house itself.

I told Anselmo to send a messenger to the village where Severina had lived. All her relatives to the third degree must come to the house in the early morning.

We had fresh eggplants, bitter melons. Anselmo had a pig butchered. I was tired. I had a long talk with Delfin in the car, all those three hours from Manila to San Quentin. He was closer to me now. And that night, he would sleep with me in one of the two air-conditioned rooms.

After dinner, Angela asked Delfin to help her with her homework. She had brought along a lot of it, and indeed she was not good at arithmetic. Not only was Delfin good at math, he was also excellent in composition, which would be an asset when he would prepare those briefs for the courts. He had earned a little money, as he had already explained, writing reports for some of his classmates. I was in bed, dozing, when Corito came in, locked the door, and extracted from me her usual pleasure. She did all the work, my mind was elsewhere and, sometimes, I could hear Angela's laughter down the hall. It was also the first time I heard Delfin laugh.

In a while, Delfin came to our room. I was in bed reading progress reports. He stripped down to his jockey shorts, displaying an Adonis physique; his torso, chest and arms exuded power, hard masculinity, reminding me of my own youth. And on his neck dangled this necklace—

I had seen it before. I stood up and went to him. "Your mother gave you this," I said, fingering the triangle. It was smooth to my touch. I remembered it as whitish, but now it was completely reddish-brown, with a soft lustre like gold.

"Yes, sir," Delfin said.

"To protect you from misfortune, from evil . . ."

He smiled rather sheepishly, I think. "Yes, sir. That was what my mother said. Especially since I come from Siquijor."

I nodded, recalling the brief profile of the island and its infestation with witchcraft.

Peace and well-being soon lulled me to sleep. I also dreamed, which rarely happens now. Sometimes I note down these dreams in some vague expectation that a good psychoanalyst might go over them and find in them aspects of my personality that have been secreted under an external patina of iron perseverance and business acumen. In this dream, I was a boy and I was in some field chasing grasshoppers. I had a bag already filled with them, and there was another boy, a peasant, who was behind me, also catching grasshoppers, and the boy was no other than Delfin. He said he would eat the grasshoppers as his mother had very little food in their house. I was filled with pity and gave him all the grasshoppers I had caught. I started to cry. I did not know people ate them and I was just catching them for fun . . . end of dream.

In reality, I know Filipinos eat grasshoppers. Even the Japanese do. Now I am again digressing because I have come to one of my favorite delights—food. Not just good food but interesting food, perhaps the only pleasure left in later years when the muscles are palsied but not the palate.

When I was a boy, a locust plague hit Nueva Ecija, among the most infested areas being San Quentin. The tenants were ecstatic instead of being apprehensive that the insects would devour their plants. With all sorts of traps and mosquito nets, they caught the locusts by the sack and sold them as far as Manila. One of the hacienda workers brought half a sack to Sta. Mesa but only I and the maids ate them, fried in vinegar, crispy and crunchy like *chitcharon*.

Our most fastidious gourmets are the Pampangos—they eat

crickets, too. All my cooks—you guessed it—are from Pampanga.

I have tried a lot of exotic food most Filipinos wouldn't touch. Ann Lee's father became a good friend—now there's a real connoisseur. It was he who introduced me to chicken feet, duck tongue and web, dog, civet cat in Chinese wine, the gamy flavor subdued, anteater and, of course, in the winter, snake soup. I've tried rattlesnake in Albuquerque; bear steak in Anchorage; moose, elk and reindeer in Stockholm; turtle meat in Malacca and, in Japan, whale sushi—its flavor is strong and fishy—and that special kamikaze sashimi, the poisonous blowfish. Its subtle taste is not worth dying for. And in Cotabato, crocodile filet—its texture is like tough chicken meat. Kangaroo tail soup in Melbourne—it's just like oxtail soup. And those beautiful Sydney oysters! No lime, no hot sauce, just its pristine taste. Chew it just a little to let its delicate flavor tease your palate, then let it glide down your throat smoothly, like the caress of an aged single malt whiskey. I am sorry to hear they are soon to become inedible because of pollution.

My most interesting eating adventure, however, was right here in the Philippines. I have mentioned earlier and at some length my interest in the welfare of our ethnic minorities—they are the poorest and most exploited of our people. I had heard of the health problems of the Dumagats in the Sierra Madre range so, on my own, I flew there by helicopter with my medical team. They had so much to do, I found out: goiter for lack of iodized salt, skin diseases, malnutrition, tuberculosis. We were high up and deep in the mountain range, in a valley that was far from the sea. I had not figured on the out-of-season typhoon that isolated us for almost a week as the helicopter couldn't come and supply us. We had to eat what the Dumagats had—plenty of vegetables, camote and dried wild pig and deer meat. We were cold, often wet, but our appetites were excellent. Never before had dried meat tasted so good.

One afternoon they brought in a big buck they had trapped and so we had fresh meat that night. It was very bland because they simply boiled it with camotes without salt. There was more meat than we could eat so I asked what they would do with the rest.

Dry it, they said.

The storm lifted that same afternoon. The following day, the sun emerged bright and steady on the verdant valley. The deer meat was laid out in the sunlight in neat strips. And everyone in the village, including the children and the women, urinated on it.

16

Wh23en I woke up, the sun was already splashing all over the room. Delfin was no longer in his bed, and when I went out, it seemed they had had breakfast, too, for there was only one plate—mine—on the breakfast table. The cook came and gave me my cup of coffee. All of them, she said, were at the other end of the lot. There were people there, she said, from some village.

I hurried with my fried rice, boneless *bangus,* fried tapa and sliced tomatoes. At the other end of the wide yard, close to the old stable, a small crowd had gathered and I recognized Delfin at once—taller than all the rest—and Angela beside him. Corito had stayed in the house. More than two dozen of them—they had all come from the village, all relatives of Severina, farmers in their shabby clothes, most of them barefoot, dark-skinned children but with good teeth, and that shy smile of peasants. Delfin was talking to them in his heavily accented Tagalog and they seemed amused. Angela beside him was listening. When I approached, all talk stopped and the villagers suddenly became quiet, greeting me at first, then looking down as if they were ashamed to meet my gaze. I did not belong there so I told Delfin to continue and I turned to go. The moment I turned, the ebullient babble resumed.

Only much, much later did I learn that this wasn't Delfin's first trip to San Quentin, that he had already visited several times. And as the *encargado* told me later on, Delfin had been giving money to Hirap, Severina's village.

I asked Delfin afterward why he never told me.

"You did not ask me, sir," he said simply. It was just like him, never volunteering information unless asked.

I had revealed too much of myself to my son. My son! This was contrary to what my father had told me. In dealing with people, never be close to anyone, the members of your immediate family excepted. Know the weaknesses of others but never let them know yours. Such a lesson had served me well in business, but with Delfin, I was truly a father seeking closeness, companionship. He had already shown me his independence and, in the hacienda, his feelings for his relatives he did not know till recently. He was close to them, those farmers, and I envied them, for I could never feel close to my second cousins, to my uncles and aunts, and to their daughters who have tried to seduce me, to their sons in my employ who expect to get a piece of the cake when I pass away. A vain hope, for I knew in their fawning attention only their greed. They resented my aloofness, my careful distancing from them and, now, I was surrendering myself to this boy who shunned me, who perhaps in his innermost being not only resented me but hated me as well.

What did my dear Severina teach him? I tried to recall my conversations with her, but I was so young then, and there was so little substance in our talks, enthused as I was only with her beauty, dark though she was, in her unquestioning submission to my demands. Father must have given her some money when she left, I never found out how much, but knowing my father, I am sure it was not enough for Severina and her son to live on. And they were in this far-flung island, this Siquijor, away from San Quentin and the sustenance that relatives could give them.

We were still in San Quentin when I told Delfin not to blame an unhappy childhood on me. I said this, noting that the children from the village of Severina all had happy faces.

"But I did not have an unhappy childhood, sir," Delfin quickly replied. "I always had enough to eat. Mother worked very hard . . ."

"What did she do?"

"She had a sister there who had married a local farmer. She helped on the farm first, then she opened a small store. She sold dried fish. I helped. I worked hard because she worked very hard."

We returned to Manila Sunday afternoon. I felt I had become closer to Delfin in those two days and yet not truly close enough, for though he was quick to answer my questions, he spoke to me without the familiarity that sons have with their fathers, the same familiarity that Angela had with me. It was she, however, who became truly close to Delfin and it seemed he was fond of her, too. Corito sat beside me in the rear and Angela chose to sit beside Delfin in the front seat with the driver.

We reached Diliman in the early evening. Delfin did not want us to take him to where he lived—a small middle-class house owned by a city hall official who, to earn some extra money, had rented out three of the rooms on the lower floor to students. We let him off a block away. He bent down for Angela to kiss him on the cheek. She had elicited a promise from him to help with her homework again.

🕱

Now, the witchcraft in Siquijor fascinated me. I asked Professor Adda Bocano from the University of the Philippines to visit; he was my consultant on our indigenous peoples. Early enough, he had made a map of the islands defining the areas where the different tribes lived.

To authenticate his social studies, he had lived in a Tondo slum for six months, worked as a room boy in one of the popular love motels in Pasig—and saw two very embarrassed colleagues there. Once, according to another story, a relative on a Friday novena at the Quiapo church saw Professor Bocano in tatters begging at the church door. Shocked, the relative had excitedly drawn aside the persevering scholar, who asked her to keep quiet. "Had times become so bad that you have become a beggar? Here, this five hundred pesos is all I have now!"

I had always found him enlightening and, that evening in my penthouse, we talked about black magic, the aswangs of the Visayas and other folk beliefs that have persisted even in urban Manila.

"How did the witchcraft in Siquijor originate?"

"Many years ago," he explained, "during the early days of the galleons, some Filipino seamen got stranded in Mexico. They strayed in the Caribbean, to the island of Haiti, and there they learned about voodoo practices. Some returned—they were from Siquijor, and on the island, they put to practice what they had learned in Haiti."

I sat back, sipping my cognac, amazed at his story.

"But mind you," Professor Bocano said, and shook a finger at me. "This is not documented. This is folk belief. There has been an effort in Silliman University to be scientific about it. In the museum there are some artifacts of this witchcraft."

"Do you believe in it?"

He smiled. "When I see the empirical evidence, then I have no choice. The truth is, if witchcraft is embedded in a particular culture, its efficacy is soon taken for granted."

"The witches, are there women?"

"Very few," Profesor Bocano explained. "Most of them are males. But the aswang—"

I remembered vaguely that the aswang, too, came from the Visayas, a malevolent creature who hovered at night over the homes of pregnant women and with her long tongue sucked the blood of the fetus.

"The story is that they come from Panay island. Mostly women. At night, the upper portion of their bodies is separated from the waist down; then they fly. If anyone comes across the separate lower half and sprinkles it with salt, the aswang will not be able to resume its human shape. It dies."

Professor Bocano was silent for a while, his eyes half-closed as if in deep thought. Then his face lit up. "But do not think of our women only in this manner. In our past, in our tradition, they were also leaders, warriors. And most of all, healers and priestesses—the link between the spiritual and the temporal . . ."

I thought of Severina, my sweet and poignant memories of her, and all the more did I realize how much I had loved her and, at the same time, how unfeeling and crass I had been.

"How does a stranger—someone who visits Siquijor—protect himself?"

Again, that noncommittal smile. "You are not supposed to leave behind anything that you have used. A lock of your hair, a bit of fingernail—these can be used to cast a spell on you. . . . There are charms, of course, to ward off such spells, amulets, pendants. Similar to those sold on the sides of Quiapo church."

I did not press for more details; I was acutely remembering the pendant Severina wore, which now adorned Delfin's chest. Did I need one myself?

I tried to see Delfin more often, once a month. He did not avoid me but he did not welcome my presence, for he was always in a hurry to get away. His suits had long been delivered but I never saw him wear them or the Italian shoes from Francesco's. He had bought instead a pair of jeans that was now his uniform.

I could see that he did not like going to the Polo Club, so every time I took him to lunch or dinner, it was at some inconspicuous restaurant near the university or, if Angela came along, in Sta. Mesa, where he stayed longer after dinner or lunch. When it was time for him to go, the car always took him to where he wished, but the driver said he did not go beyond the main street, where he would then board a bus or a jeepney.

I opened a checking account for him at a bank on the campus so he did not have to receive any cash from me. I was also waiting for any report on amorous developments, but my aide said there weren't any, just the usual group dates with classmates and with some girls from nearby Maryknoll. I started worrying about his being a homosexual, although his shadow did not think so. He simply was too devoted to his studies and, indeed, all through those years in law school, he kept his scholarship. That took some doing and I was truly proud of him.

Come February 14 in his senior year, when young people celebrated Valentine's Day, I found he had no party to go to. I had invited four of my prettiest young nieces, none of whom I had fornicated with. We went to the Polo Club for dinner and some dancing. I had asked him to put on one of the tropical suits Francesco had made, but he came in the same old khakis, freshly laundered for sure, and a cheap synthetic fiber barong Tagalog. He had also had a haircut. I made sure that he joined us—I had him picked up at his residence by one of the drivers, and when he arrived, Angela, growing up very fast, rushed to the door and greeted him with a loud kiss.

"Delf!" she exclaimed. "You are very handsome!"

She led him to our table. Corito and the girls were chatting happily in Spanish but all conversation stopped when Delfin arrived at the table. It must have been obvious to him, to Corito and to Angela that the four girls were there so he could meet them. The introductions over, they vied for his attention, chattering in English with him but switching to Spanish when they talked among themselves. I now realized by the expression on his face that Delfin understood every word, but he refused to speak with them, or to me and Corito, in Spanish. It was only with Angela, I learned later, when it was just the two of them, that he spoke Spanish with some diffidence. Dutifully, he danced with all my pretty nieces, and took them back to our table, impassive and silent. Then he brightened up when Angela asked him to dance with her. She was around ten, and tall; she danced awkwardly, gawkily, and we looked at them, extremely amused. She seemed, however, to be very happy. Indeed, she would tell me later that it was the most beautiful Valentine's Day she had ever had.

But for Angela, it was a disastrous evening for Delfin; he ignored the other young ladies completely and barely talked with them, preferring instead to talk to Angela and to Corito and, occasionally, to me.

I wondered what was wrong with the girls—they were all good-looking, three of them seniors at the Assumption, one had just finished college in California. They were sophisticated and adept in all the social graces. No, there was nothing wrong with them. Delfin, reared in that village in Siquijor, was still a country boy and did not fit in. By nine, after dinner, Angela said she was sleepy and wanted to go home. Corito wanted to stay.

"I will accompany her," Delfin said. He must have been so bored he wanted to leave.

I decided to leave, too, so I could be with my son. Corito would take care of the girls; there were many bachelors at the Club, the girls could easily find dancing partners.

The three of us sat in the rear. Angela, in the middle, was already asleep, her head resting on my arm. Could she be listening if I talked with Delfin about women? I asked what was wrong with the girls I invited.

"They are snobs, sir," he said flatly. "I know their kind. Some are in my own school."

What could I say? Maybe I was a snob myself, since I did not see anything wrong with them.

"I had hoped that you would find at least one of them interesting," I said. "I had invited them just so you could meet them."

"Thank you, sir," he said quickly. "I know that. I am sorry that I had to call them snobs . . ."

"Maybe you are right," I said. Then I asked if there was a girl in Siquijor.

"Yes, sir," he said quickly. In glimpses of his face lighted by passing cars and streetlamps, I could see he was smiling.

"Would you like to tell me about her?"

"There isn't much to tell, sir. She finished high school but couldn't go on to college. Her family could not afford it."

"She—you, what are your plans?"

"None, sir. How could . . ." But he did not go on.

"You wanted to say something."

Angela stirred and we stopped talking. After a while, Angela seemed to be asleep again.

We had reached Sta. Mesa. "Carry your cousin to her room," I said. He scooped Angela up in his arms and carried her up the steps.

I wanted to know more about the girl in Siquijor. We went to the library. I asked one of the maids who was up to bring some cold cuts. I hadn't eaten much at the Club. From the bar, I got myself a glass of Pedro Domecq, another for Delfin. I suspected he had never had brandy, so I told him to sip it.

I sprang the question without warning. "Are you still a virgin, *hijo?*"

He laughed slightly. No tone of embarrassment in his reply, but he was not looking at me when he spoke. His eyes were on the shelves bulging with books, some of them leather-bound.

"No, sir."

"That girl in Siquijor?"

He nodded, but did not speak.

"You did not get her pregnant?"

He shook his head.

"You owe her some loyalty then."

"More than that, sir."

"Well, you are in Manila now. Here the temptations are everywhere. But I am sure you know how to protect yourself? Condoms and all those things. Disease can be infectious. You will be hurting not just yourself but others if you are not careful." I was now speaking of myself, with authority, with the hope that this boy would not make the same mistake I had.

"I know well enough of that, sir," he assured me. "It is really better to abstain, and to keep away from the professionals."

I was relieved. I was finally having a man-to-man talk with my son and, that evening, I felt as close to him as any father could to his son. Knowing, too, how strong-willed he was, he would surely be able to stay celibate, or if he ever surrendered to the flesh, he would be dressed for the occasion.

▨

Did I trust too much his sense of personal discipline, propriety? Only time, of course, would tell how he would stand when finally subjected to the test.

I had fallen asleep, pleased and at peace with the world, confident that my relations with my son were growing closer, warmer, and that I had slowly widened the once narrow corridor where we both trod. It must have been long past midnight—I was wakened by Corito who had returned from the dance. In the dimness, I could make her out as she slipped into my bed and lay beside me, still in her party frock. She kissed me on the cheek, a sisterly kiss, smelling a little of wine, and feminine fragrance. She had put on some weight, was now buxom, but still very good-looking. She was not going to extract her pleasure from me tonight—if that was her intent, she would have come in her negligee with nothing underneath. There were times when I really liked her beside me like this, comfortable, undemanding, and full of domestic chitchat.

"Did you notice that Delfin and I danced twice tonight?" she asked.

I had noticed, of course.

"Oye, Carling," she said, "you know what I did? I gave Delfin a terrific hard-on."

I turned to her. I could not believe what I heard.

Her hand wandered down my stomach, slipped under my pajama and held the stem firmly, tightly. She croaked, "I rubbed against his groin. I could feel it really hard, and he pressed it to me . . ."

"I don't believe it," I said, not reacting at all to her caress.

She drew her hand away and sat up.

"Ask him," she said. "Ask him," she repeated with a gloating laugh as she headed for the door.

17

I will be asked by that supreme inquisitor—no, not God, but my own conscience: What meaning have you given your life? I must retort: Should life have any meaning other than it be lived pleasurably? This is not a hedonistic attitude; all over the world, people are searching for objects of belief; some see it in politics, in religion, but this attempt to reach out for eternity— in a sense, this is what this searching is all about—is bound to fail because eternity does not exist; the pristine nature of things change, and it is this inevitability of change that, from the beginning, we must always be conscious of. But human nature is, by itself, unchanging, the lust and the greed commingled with the saintly attitudes and selflessness of those who are so inclined. And I? Look not just at myself, inutile now and in this hapless condition. Look at what this mind and this body have achieved! I have bequeathed to this nation progress, fed hundreds, gave them and their families their reasons for being. Don't talk to me about justice—I know it not as an abstraction, but in the fullness of my deeds. Those yammering cru-

saders, those who have lambasted me, what have they themselves done? I scorn them, ignore them, regard them as despi-
cable cockroaches hiding in dark, stinking crevices of oblivion.
They could not do what I have done, and knowing this, I stand
above them all, superior not so much because of my genes but
because I have used my wealth and my power in my best moral
lights.

At this juncture, perhaps, I should explain my continued interest in prostitution not as a social problem but as an instrument by which I could further my influence, my interests. I have
already stated how I set up a travel agency. It served me and my
companies very well. But above such a service, two of my talent
scouts recruited girls from the Continent, not for some brothel
such as my father operated in Pasay, but for the social lions of
Manila, the powerful politicians and businessmen who wanted
sexual variety and at the same time would be assured of complete privacy. They could well afford the prettiest women—all
of them non-Filipinos—which my agency recruited and, God,
I made them pay! It was for this reason that these aides were always in Australia, the United States and Europe, in Spain and
Italy particularly—for it is in these two countries where they obtained the best girls, who visited as tourists and were billeted in
houses in Makati or in the five-star Manila hotels.

"*Hijo*," I told Delfin, "if the compulsion comes, let me
know. I have so many connections. Beautiful women, all of
them very clean—I can assure you of that."

I had become a pimp to my own son, but I was determined
that he suffer no disease as I had done. I may have shocked
him, but it was common enough for the rich fathers I knew to
initiate their boys into this domain that is woman with the girls
I had procured from Europe.

❊

When I learned that Delfin was giving away almost all of his
money, I decided to limit the amount I sent to his bank ac-

count, but there would always be enough for him to fall back on. Yes, that was it, I was his fallback position even if he did not admit it. Perhaps his knowledge that I was there with the safety net emboldened him, gave him a sense of security. I always demanded this when I went into a new enterprise; if it failed, what was our fallback position? Actually, I did not bother too much with it, although I made sure it was always there. With my bulging portfolios, I had great liquidity, stocks and bonds in the international market, U.S. treasury notes, hard currencies squirreled away and earning slowly but surely, and yes, gold bullion, too.

May I say here, now, how much I admired the Leader, particularly after he declared martial law. I was not in his anointed inner circle; I am not Ilokano or a classmate. But I did not want him to consider me an enemy either. Even before he grabbed so many enterprises, I had already protected my flanks, and not only in my friendship with him and his cronies—hah! how many times were the European beauties in my stable his for the asking. I had connected with the Japanese, the Americans and the Germans; they were a safeguard against his greed. And whenever I was asked, I was also prepared to give.

I said I admired him; he would have been the complete entrepreneur, taking over established businesses with verve and premeditation—the very virtues that I would have possessed more of. Of course, what he did with what he grabbed, that I did not approve of. Whatever one may say about my massive investments abroad, I have not neglected this country, not out of loyalty, mind you, but because this is where I live. Capital, like water, seeks its own level. Wherever there's profit to be made, it will go there.

Delfin was now on my mind often. I had decided to mold him into an heir fit to take over my empire. That is not an exaggeration. It is an empire of sorts that stretches from the Philippines to Europe, to America and, of course, Asia, too.

Not in the grand manner of the Greek tycoons, the Arab sheiks or the Sultan of Brunei, but on a more modest scale, though global just the same.

All my companies were earning and my food-processing factory was ready to go regional. All were directed by my holding company, Cobello y Cia. I had an intelligence operation that kept me informed about my own people, the opposition and those in power. Every bit fed to me was double-checked and triple-checked. When someone's head was cut off, the victim always knew he had it coming. I never did the executions myself. Always there were subalterns who did it for me. I had learned from my father how to protect myself by having others do the dirty work. And they did it skillfully, gladly, for all of them were rewarded well. *Divide et empere!* It is an easy game to play and those who play it must always be sure they will not be dragged down by the undertow.

Liberal arts for Delfin took only three years, not four. He was now entering law school. He landed a job at the Nojok law office as a researcher, a job he was very proud to have found, for I learned later that he worshipped this lawyer, this Nojok.

I did not like Nojok at all, his nationalist posturing, his continuous harping about corruption in government. In a sense, I was glad when the Leader imprisoned him; he should have kept him there longer. Not only was he bad for the Americans with whom I had very lucrative relations but for business in general. In the earlier years, he had run out of the country a business associate, Alfred Dangmount. Alfred had come to the Philippines as an American GI and had stayed on after Liberation to set up several businesses. The man had vision. I know, because I was involved in his plans to set up factories. He had planned on making this country self-sufficient and productive in textiles and, together, we had begun ramie plantations in Mindanao and cotton in the Ilocos.

We would have been the world's foremost producer of this

magic fiber, ramie, but this Nojok hounded Dangmount. What wrong did Dangmount do? He was no different from us, whether Spanish or Chinese mestizos. He just blabbered too much, and said nasty things, such as he could buy any public official, which was true anyway. And so he went and, of course, the businesses that he started were soon taken over by us. I worried, perhaps unnecessarily, that Nojok would also go after people like me, but, fortunately, people like him, these crusaders, do not last long in government. They are soon booted out because they go against the grain, because they turn the faucets off when so many politicians are thirsty.

These do-gooders, these pseudo saints, when will they ever understand that it is this symbiotic relationship between business and government that makes quicker progress possible? Look at Japan's rise to economic dominance in such a short time! Nojok's populist nationalism also bothered me; one of our best assets has always been cheap labor, be it rural or urban. He was always pleading for social justice, for the expulsion of the American bases, for honesty in government—all of these anathema to my own interests. And now, my son was working for him!

Yet I should have expected it. I recall an early conversation about why Delfin was going to take up law. As a lawyer, he had a ready niche in my business. I could see that. Angela could not do the job, given her poor physical condition and being a woman and so young at that. And what was his explanation then? That there was a lot of injustice in Siquijor.

He was going to be Sir Galahad, a knight on a white horse, with youthful idealism that would be tempered by age, by the reality of the world outside that campus. Former student leaders, radicals in their college days, but now, in fine summer suits in Makati, timorous conservatives, work for moneybags like myself. Surely Delfin would mature and, in anticipation of that, I had drawn my will for the third time, made many corrections

on the first that named Corito and Angela as the major bene-
ficiaries.

I am convinced of Delfin's common sense. His ancestry will
compel him to do as I have done. When the responsibility of
running the estate passed on to me upon Father's death, I had
to be equal to the challenge, I could not have spent all that
fortune gambling, because I didn't gamble, or on luxurious
living, because there was more than enough for that, or on
women—I didn't have to go far to have that hunger appeased.

So will it be with Delfin—and, thank God, he is a lawyer and
better equipped than I was at his age. By himself, he cannot destroy an organization that has its own momentum, a machine
that performs with the least interference from he who owns it.
Will he make the engine stop? He is full of goodwill—he will
need all the money he can to fulfill that goodwill in his heart.
And when he realizes this, then he will also realize that he cannot kill the goose that lays those precious golden eggs!

He had derided the Rockefellers and the robber barons. He
cannot be accused of hypocrisy—he can very well follow their
do-gooding example—and what I have built will then be sanctified by him with a halo of philanthropy.

And Angela, my dear Angela, ten, twelve years younger than
he, will be his beacon. All through her young years, I have told
her that wealth begets wealth begets wealth. She understands
this logic. She is not a Cobello for nothing.

☒

Four years and Angela had bloomed in many ways, but she was
still frail, in need of constant medical care. She had become
asthmatic and she suffered the omnipresent dust, the damp-
ness, the slight variations of weather. But she was brave, determined, taking up sports that were not strenuous and following
the regimen prescribed for her. At fourteen, she was simply
beautiful, her hair glossy and brownish in the light, her eyes

alight and large. Indeed, she deserved her name—she had an angelic countenance and a voice so clear, so limpid, it was such a pleasure to listen to her. Maybe I exaggerate her attributes.

It was from Angela now that I got the latest news about my son, for all through intermediate school, Angela visited him at least once a week at his boardinghouse in Diliman. She brought him things, food, fruits, candy, whatever she fancied. "He is a very good teacher, Tito," she told me.

I was very glad they had developed such an affectionate relationship. "He is not uncomfortable with your visits?"

Angela puckered. "No, he is fun to be with."

She knew enough not to visit Delfin in any of the big cars, the Mercedes—two of which were new additions in the garage. She was driven in an old battered Ford that the cook used when going to the market.

She described Delfin's room. "It's tiny, with just a chair, a table and an iron cot. We sit on the cot when he teaches me."

I have never been inside that house, that room no larger than the bathrooms in the house, but it was clean and airy. How I wished I could tell my Angela that Delfin was her half brother, not her cousin as she believed. The fullest sense of family, its profound emotional pleasure was beginning to enthrall me, give me an exalted purpose, and not just the business sallies where I had always triumphed. I was beginning to luxuriate in the feeling and Angela had made it all possible.

Delfin flourished in law school. I was not surprised at all when he topped the bar—that was what his classmates and his professors expected. In all those seven years, although I had often asked him, he had never traveled abroad. I would have brought him with me on my trips to Europe or the United States, or even to nearby Hong Kong, where I went as a matter of course, and to Tokyo, too. But he had refused, always saying he had to maintain his scholarship although it was no longer necessary for his sustenance. And then he started working in that infernal law office.

It was Angela again who convinced him to vacation in Hong Kong. Corito came along so that we could have some family life, although I must add that she had now become almost intolerable, demanding my presence, bothering me in my work.

Angela chose the penthouse in the condo named after her, not in the old Kowloon Tong block that was built earlier; the condo's magnificent view of the busy harbor was unhindered by the new apartment blocks burgeoning all over the place. I had carefully chosen the lot when I was looking for a place to invest in and Ann Lee had located it. It was October and cool, the sky untarnished. Delfin had not put on weight in all these years, but I had. He finally wore the suits that Francesco had cut for him, and he truly looked patrician, urbane, a young up-and-coming professional. They did not call them yuppies in those days—1965 and the last days of Macapagal as president. The Philippines was still prosperous, the Leader had yet to come and set back the nation.

Hong Kong was changing. The old brick buildings had been torn down and, in their place, monoliths of stone and glass had sprung up. More apartment blocks had also risen on the peak. Mine stood out, as did my building in Manila, and the house in Dasmariñas, for all were designed by Tanga, the famous Japanese architect. He had come to Manila and stayed here for a couple of months, and also in Hong Kong for a month before the actual designs of the buildings were even started.

Filipino architects? Not one of them has the intelligence and the imagination to define Philippine architecture itself, to understand the need to merge function and form in consonance with climate, available materials, Philippine aesthetics. All of them are copycats, depending on innovations and styles from abroad. All you have to do is look at the morass in Makati and all those California bungalows there!

Delfin's first trip out of the country, and I watched him keenly, the unfeigned wonder on his face, how he noticed everything. Angela took him sightseeing in the New Territories and on long walks along the shop-lined streets of Kowloon. She also visited the apartment block there, the three units rented out to American businessmen.

I was now sure Delfin was much closer to me, his resentment slowly vanishing. Angela did this. My ever precious Angela, conceived in sin and now a delight to watch. The cool weather brought the rose to her cheeks. She was much taller than her mother and she moved about, in spite of her frailty, with a graceful liveliness. Now, she and Delfin spoke in Spanish even in our presence. I had suspected all along that he had learned the language well but had not spoken it till he was confident. With Angela, that confidence grew.

18

We returned to Manila after a relaxed, delightful week in the crown colony. Delfin now had a better position in the law firm—he was made a junior partner. In college, he had stayed away from the demonstrations and the radical rhetoric for which the university was well known. I had wondered why, with his scholastic standing, he had refrained from student politics, not even bothering to be in the student council or on the editorial board of the college paper, which every aspiring student politician sought. I think I know the reason: finally, as a lawyer, he could take on the cases of farmers and workers who were victimized by their landlords and employers. He had not surrendered to the virtuous blather of college juveniles: he had prepared himself for action, for deeds. And I was truly bothered by the direction he had taken.

It was Angela, now that I knew he confided in her, already in high school, who kept me informed of his movements, of the lawyer Nojok himself whom Delfin worshipped. If Nojok could not go to the provinces to defend the peasants, he sent two or three lawyers, Delfin always part of the team, and these, at the expense of Nojok himself. Now Delfin would be in Mindanao defending the settlers from the loggers and banana plantation owners who had grabbed their farms. Now he was in Negros, allied with some priests and the Farmers Federation, fighting for the sugar workers. There was hardly any place he went that I did not know. I didn't even have to ask Angela anymore—she volunteered the information, knowing how interested I was in my son's doings. By this time his salary had increased and he had moved to a modest one-room apartment in Quezon City.

The Leader had already declared martial law, a master stroke that could be made only by one who had planned decisively. I have always appreciated such qualities in businessmen, and it is for this reason that I admired him. He would have been a very successful entrepreneur if he hadn't been waylaid by politics. Nojok was imprisoned for two years but, during this time, Delfin continued working, perhaps even more so than before. Nojok soon organized PLUG (Progress, Liberty Under God), a group of lawyers working voluntarily to assist the political prisoners of the dictator.

At one of those dinners at the palace, the Leader took me aside. I had known him since he was a congressman, and I called him Brod then, just as he always called me by my nickname, C.C. Or Carling, or Charlie, or sometimes Don Carlos. But when he became president, I always addressed him as Mr. President. At a dinner at the Manila Hotel, he told me to drop the Mr. President routine but I persisted, even when there were only the two of us. I think he appreciated it.

"Well, Carling, how is your son?" he asked with a smile.

My chest tightened. I was only too aware of what Delfin was doing and I am sure the Leader did not like it, just as he had no love for Nojok, although he released the man after two years in prison.

"I hope he is not giving your people problems, Mr. President," I said nervously. "I have tried to keep him in line, but he has a mind of his own."

"I know." The Leader continued smiling. Then he told an aide who was standing by to call for the chief of staff. General Beer came in, pompous in white and braid, with a generous splash of fruit salad on his chest.

"General, you know Don Carlos Cobello."

"Yes, sir," the general answered stiffly, head erect, eyes stern and unsmiling.

"You also gave me a report on his son, Delfin."

"Yes, sir."

"Well, General. Don't touch him. Leave him alone. Understand?"

"Yes, sir."

The Leader waved him away, then turned to me, his eyes crinkling with laughter. "Ah, the second generation. We really don't know what they will turn out to be. We are old friends, Carling, and you are on my side. I won't forget that." And slapping me on the shoulder, he turned to pay attention to the other guests.

I was never so relieved in my life; I had worried about Delfin getting in the way of people like General Beer—boors and automatons who, as the Leader said, would jump out the window without any question if ordered to.

✠

One day Angela came to my Makati office, her face shrouded with gloom. She said Delfin had gone to Siquijor. "He has a girlfriend there," she said. Then she told me how in the last eight years or so, he had gone to Siquijor three times, this time very worried because the girl had not written to him in four months although he wrote every so often.

I told Angela that that was where he grew up. She pouted. "Now he will get married to her." And tears began to well in her eyes. I was too dumb to realize then what had happened to her.

Delfin returned after three days. Angela was very happy, but she said Delfin was inconsolable. "I have never seen him in such anguish, Tito," she said. I decided to visit him.

I picked him up at the Nojok law office in Quezon City and we went to one of those restaurants in Timog. Angela was right; sorrow was etched deeply on his face.

"Would you like to tell me what happened?" I asked when we were finally seated.

At first, it did not seem like he wanted to talk, but after a while, the words came slowly. "I was faithful to her. I wrote to her very often, told her to wait till I was ready to support her. She couldn't wait, sir. And I cannot blame her. Eight years is much too long for any girl."

"She got married?"

"Yes, that is why she never answered my letters afterward. I hope it will be a good marriage. He is well off—he is the governor's son."

As I said, Angela did not share Delfin's loss. In no time, she told me, too, that Delfin had won another scholarship, this time to the law school at Yale.

How soon will he leave for America? But Delfin did not go. The scholarship could wait. All there was to know and do were in the Philippines. And the best teacher in the country was no other than the man he worshipped.

I began to loathe Nojok. My son looked up to him not just as a lawyer and teacher but as a paragon of virtue, committing himself to the common man. And he, a mestizo like me, although it was American genes in his system, not Spanish.

And with Nojok, my son would go to the masses, the rabble. Ah, the masses! I find them contemptible, without ambition, lazy, lying, thieving. How right my father had been! Why are they so fawning? So blatantly ingratiating? Don't they have any self-respect? They don't know how to save. Payday—and they don't report for work the day after; they spend a fortune on beer; I don't resent that, I am a major stockholder in the brewery. Tomorrow does not matter to them, only ostentation, pleasure now. And they blame us for their plight, we who give them jobs, who are making this nation grow. Yes, I have profited from their labor but I pay and pay, and pay. My workers have the most benefits compared with the pittance the Chinese and Indios give them. Rice rations, hospitalization, vacation leaves, insurance—they got all these without bargaining, without a union. And still they complain. My father and his father before him were right: do not expect gratitude, especially from these Indios. At every turn they are ingrates, traitors. *Cuedao!*

But I am now in this most pitiable condition, unable to work, to pursue the pleasures that were offered to me even without my asking. And my son, my son! Instead of coming close to me, he is moving away.

I wanted to tell him about my conversation with the Leader, that, because of my friendship with the dictator, he was safe. But I didn't, for I was sure it would only alienate him further. To know that I had such close ties with the Leader would even make him contemptuous of me. And I know people like him— they would love to go to prison themselves!

Angela, my joy, how happy I am that she cares. But does she really? I now have my doubts, too. It's her closeness to Delfin that is changing her. It is not school or even growing up. The questions she asks me now are sometimes pointed. I am sure they are all Delfin's doing. Is he turning my Angela against me, too?

I asked Angela. "The truth, *hija*. Does Delfin hate me?"

She was in my office waiting for me to put the last paper in my out tray. Only she and Corito could barge in at any time. Only they. I have given Delfin the same privilege, but he has never visited. Here I am, one of the richest men in the country, in the region even, and I am needled, anxious about how one person regards me.

Angela was in her junior year in high school; she had come in, kissed me and wanted me to take her to lunch at this new Makati restaurant that her classmates had been to the day before.

"Why ask such a question!" she exclaimed. "Delf—he is very grateful for all the things you have done for him. But he wants to make it on his own, Tito. You must understand that."

"He is indifferent then. He just tolerates me . . ."

"That is not how it is, I know. He is glad you are here, that you have recognized him. You are his last resort!"

"And what am I to you?" I was truly relieved; my assumption was correct that I was his fallback position.

Another kiss. "My first and last resort. In fact, my only resort," she whispered.

Now it was easy for me to understand his courage, his determination to be on his own. I was there with the safety net in case he failed. But was I really that important to him? His future? I remember only too well how quickly he had walked out on me when I first saw him. Surely he knew by then the magnitude of my means. Now, it was clear to him with his law background that illegitimate children had rights to the property of their parents. But he walked away! He walked away!

Then I thought of the money I had given him; he did not refuse it or deny it. Or throw it away either. He gave the money to his relatives—yes, that was the best thing to do. This meant that he would welcome any sum I would give him. He was not all that proud after all and, again, I felt some comfort with that thought.

I tried bringing Delfin to America and Europe when he did not take the Yale fellowship. Most of all, I wanted to take him to New York and to nearby New Haven so he could see the ivy league school where he should be. But again, he refused. Now PLUG had so much work to do, even on Sundays he was working.

Like his teacher and idol, he was charging into the wild thickets of corruption. He couldn't win, of course, when it was the truly powerful he finally confronted.

But first, let me sound off on some of my business ideas. I never went to business school, Harvard or Wharton, as so many of our young businessmen had done. But I have employed a few who have. Not that I consider these schools worthless; they are useful, they improve on the jargon of business and make it clearer for us who use it. Entrepreneurship is instinctive, the capacity to recognize opportunities, like I have said, long before others see them, and to exploit them. No sentimentality whatsoever here, just the simple logic of trade, the strong taking advantage of the weak, the equally simple logic of capitalism, profit.

I look at land therefore as no more than a source of profit, none of that vaulting notion about land and nation, and social justice for the peasantry. I often marvel at the naïveté of these so-called social reformers, these mealymouthed armchair revolutionaries always equating land with freedom. With me, it is production, how it can be increased. It was with this objective in mind that my planning staff, looking coldly at our agriculture, decided to go into mechanization on my rice land that was irrigated by rainfall. I would introduce cotton for export— Philippine cotton was known for its high quality long before the Spaniards came. There was demand for it locally in our textile mills. Alfred Dangmount and I had agreed on this venture earlier, did project studies that confirmed our plans. I was going into intercropping, too, where there was irrigation. We had had enough lessons from the Taiwanese. It would not be difficult. My people already had plenty of experience in mechanized farming, as all the sugarlands had long been cultivated mostly by machines. It was necessary to let go several farmers who, before they were uprooted, would be given some form of restitution to tide them over while they looked for new places of work.

I believed in this compensation not because I cared for social justice but because it was necessary. I have always believed in a healthy workforce, in its being emotionally secure, too, so it would be more efficient. The rural workers were not going to be an exception.

I did not know and it really did not matter that a few of Delfin's relatives were among those to be displaced. I only found out about it when the Nojok law office filed a case against Hacienda Esperanza.

Delfin came to me. He must have surrendered some pride to do so. It was also the first time I learned that Severina's cousin and his family were to be uprooted, and they had gone to see Delfin about it.

Sunday morning in Sta. Mesa and I could see how happy Angela was that Delfin had come. He joined us at the breakfast table on the terrace, but he had only coffee. He did not waste time. "They have been your workers all their lives, sir. Now they have nowhere to go."

I knew how important the case was for him. But I have always been judicious in making decisions. I wanted information, and he couldn't say I procrastinated. In his presence, although it was Sunday, I called up my lawyers and despatched a messenger to Nueva Ecija for the *encargado* and some members of his staff to come to Manila immediately. Delfin left the house convinced that I had acted on his behalf.

⬛

Let me state here that I knew, sooner or later, there would be land reform not because it was demanded by the farmers and their champions but because prosperity demanded it. The Leader was right in abolishing tenancy with one stroke of the pen; the absence of tenure for the peasant had been responsible not just for agrarian discontent but for low productivity; the anachronism had to end. But there must be just compensation to those who owned the land and this is where the trouble starts. What is just compensation? If the peasants are attached to the land, is the landlord less attached? But more than these sentimental considerations, look at what landholding has done to our very rich, particularly those Negros *hacenderos*. They are imbued with that calcified view of landlords, of doing nothing but waiting for the harvest and the rent. Go to any of the Manila hotel coffee shops. The landlords are there gossiping instead of working hard like I do. Take the land from them and they will be forced to work, to use their brains to create wealth.

Anselmo, the *encargado*, and two assistants arrived late in the afternoon and they told me the details. Indeed, fifty-four families would be displaced as a result of mechanization and consolidation of the land. Had they already left the hacienda? Not yet—a court order had delayed that.

Jake, my chief counsel, had to leave his golf game and had joined us for lunch in Sta. Mesa. He said the case was in the Court of Appeals. I asked him about our chances of winning, and he explained the new law on agrarian reform signed by the Leader, which we had not broken. Compensation was going to be paid to the tenants, and if they stayed on they would be hired as workers.

"We have a fifty-fifty chance," Jake said.

It was such a trivial matter about which I should not have bothered, but it was now important only because of Delfin. If we had a fifty-fifty chance, with Nojok as our opponent, the possibility of our losing was great. My lawyers are corporate specialists and now that they were handling an agrarian case— a highly political one at that—I had some doubts about their ability.

There are always ways, of course, by which we could win and

even reverse the decisions of the lower courts. Should I let things be and make Delfin and his relatives happy? It was so easy to do—noblesse oblige again. I had done it so many times and it always gave me some pleasure, for it made me less a monster before my own people.

Then it occurred to me that Delfin needed a lesson, to know the reality of power, of wealth. I would teach him that.

I went to Europe, to America, for three months, to have my physical check-up in Houston, to firm up deals in Germany. In Hong Kong, Ann Lee was waiting; I spent a week with her. In San Francisco, a pretty niece was waiting. I took her everywhere I went in the United States. In Frankfurt, another niece. Finally, Tokyo, and Corito and Angela joined me there.

In Tokyo, Jake reported to me on the hacienda case. The Court of Appeals decided soon enough in my favor. As expected, the Nojok law office elevated the case to the Supreme Court, where it could have languished forever. But in a month—such unusual speed indeed!—the highest court in the land decided also in my favor.

The day after we returned to Sta. Mesa, Delfin came. Defeat, dejection, were all over his countenance. He asked if I knew what had happened to the hacienda case and I lied, saying I had yet to see the report of the lawyers. I implied that the case was not all that important, that I had returned to a pile of work that needed my attention more.

It was the first time I saw my son break down and cry. Then he restrained himself. "Sir, I know—we know you bought the justices all the way to the Supreme Court. All the way. No case could have moved so fast as it did. I know now that the lives of people not important to you do not matter at all."

I was glad that in the library where we were talking neither Angela nor Corito were present. I barked at him, "*Hijo,* put in that narrow brain of yours that no one tangles with me and expects to win. No one!"

"I know, sir," he said softly. "You have so much wealth, so much power, you can buy everyone." And without another word, he turned and left.

I half-expected that reaction, risked it even. I then summoned my hacienda staff and my lawyers again. I will now give away a bit of the hacienda, the very same rice land that would be mechanized. Those who were tilling the land can now have it—Delfin's relatives most of all. Give it away literally, for though there was a small mortgage, it was insignificant from my point of view. Not the tenants—the installments were small, but I knew they would not be able to maintain the payments.

The surveyors came and, again, in only a few months, the tenants got title to the land—faster than any touted government program. The education of Delfin was continuing. He could not fault me with being unjust. Not anymore. But now, he resisted every effort I made to see him.

19

Again, the old and nagging thought bores into me like some purposeful and avenging hex, condemning me, taunting me, and, again, I cry out—Severina, forgive me, lift this curse that you have cast upon me so that I will be free again.

Oh, that I could release this atrophied body from its own prison, for the mind to wallow again in the luxury of sensuality now that the flesh cannot.

I look around me and remember all the pleasures I have had and can no longer enjoy. So now, it is only the eyes that can absorb what is left. The sense of smell, of taste, are laden with possibilities, but even these I must reach for. Without my hands and feet?

I begin to question my sanity. I turn in my mind over and over, a dozen plowshares ripping into the earth to expose the worm—is there one wayward word I have uttered, any action no longer commanded by sheer logic, by untarnished ethical consideration? But how can the mind be detached from itself? How can an eye look within itself? This self—how distant and infinitely incongruous it always is unto itself that demands self-dissection. Or is it self-destruction?

My hands—inert, bloated, nerveless—how I long for them to feel once more the soft, pneumatic texture of a female breast, to grasp a pliant, fragrant body against my own, to feel the whole smooth contour of that living flesh pressed, welded to my own quivering flesh. I do it in my shriveled mind's eye, remembering Severina most of all, glorifying again in remembered tastes and scents.

Severina, forgive me!

❦

The shock of my life came the year Angela finished high school. As a graduation gift, I bought an emerald necklace for her at Bulgari's and arranged for her and Corito to vacation in Europe; the houses in Spain were seldom used—they would stay for a month in the spring and early summer when Europe was truly beautiful. I had planned on sending Delfin with them, if I could see him. We had a small dinner at the Polo Club to which Angela invited a dozen of her friends, most of them since grade school. She had often spoken about her lawyer cousin to them and, now, she anxiously turned to the dining hall entrance every time there was a new arrival.

She was regal in a cream-white taffeta dress, around her neck the new emerald necklace. When we were having dessert and Delfin had not yet appeared, she gave up.

In the car back to Sta. Mesa, seated between Corito and me, she started to cry. "He didn't care. He didn't care," she repeated in Spanish. And then, turning to her mother: "I love Delfin, Mama."

This cannot be! This must not be! I should have known—all the signals were hoisted before me. Why did I not recognize them? It was not just infatuation when she was a child; she had grown up nurturing the feeling.

Corito's silence revealed her unspoken disapproval, her shock as well. Was our sin coming back to mock us? Then Corito spoke softly, guardedly, expressing my own thoughts.

"You are cousins, Angie dearest."

Her sobbing stopped. She turned to me, then to her mother. "I couldn't help myself, Mama. It just happened."

"What does Delfin say?" I finally asked.

"He knows! He knows! He said I must stop my juvenile infatuation. I am too young—and like you said, he also repeated it, we are cousins. But I know he loves me, too. Once, he kissed me . . ."

Fear, consternation—all such unexplainable feelings clawed at me.

"But now, I am not sure," Angela said softly. "He didn't come and I wanted so much to introduce him to my friends. They know about my feelings."

I tried comforting her. "It is me Delfin did not want to see, not you," I said, but she would have none of it.

At home, close to midnight, Corito and I went to Angela's room. She was still up, in her party dress, looking pensively out into the night, at the city below glittering with light.

I had had a harried talk earlier with Corito. She knew all the arguments. I let her speak. "Angie, dearest, do you know what it means to be married to a cousin? Look at yourself first, already so frail. Look at the children of the Danteses. Most of them misfits, crazies. And all because cousins in their family had intermarried."

"I know, Mama," she said. "But if Delfin wants me, I will take that risk."

"Besides, he is much, much older than you. You are so young," I said, "so protected from the world . . ."

Before I could finish, she said. "But Delf is not. He will protect me. And I am seventeen!" She stood up, all that youth and shimmering beauty, the emerald necklace gilding the lily. "And, Tito, you think I know so little of reality. That's not true, Tito. Delf helped open my eyes. And I am very observant."

What could I say? This was my Angela, now grown up, now making decisions on her own without coaching, without us pushing. I wanted to know how far the relationship had gone, the intimacy. Corito would find that out and she would tell me.

She came to my room soon after. It was very rare for us now to embrace. Somehow I had managed to distance myself from her and her appetites. She did not know I had paid some of those handsome young gigolos who entertained her, unable as she was to bear a child. She knew I preferred much younger women, my nieces, for instance, and she also had become aware that she had become flabby with middle age. But she still smelled the same, all sweet femininity, and her closeness always brought me a sense of comfort—that is, when she was not raging with jealousy.

I should not have bothered at all with Angela's virtue. She had tried, but Delfin had resisted and that took some doing, knowing how beautiful my Angela is.

We plotted. She and Angela would go on with their European vacation. Corito would be on the lookout for eligible men in Spain. I knew Isabel Pres, the former Manila girl who was now a social butterfly in Spain, having married and divorced three distinguished and rich Spaniards. I told Corito to get Isabel to introduce Angela to prominent bachelors. Isabel would do that in payment for past favors. Corito would also convince Angela to remain in New York (where I had just bought a Park Avenue condo) or in that house in San Francisco, take a course in business administration in preparation for the time when she would have a hand in running the business. I had lectured her, impressed upon her the responsibility that she would shoulder. I was not going to live forever.

I do not know what transpired between her and Delfin. She saw him before they left and she did not seem so melancholy anymore.

✠

Corito left Angela in San Francisco as planned. It was not difficult for her to enroll at Mills. Her grades were good and I was very happy, for she would now be away from Delfin, and her chances of meeting a young man there not of Indio descent were also excellent.

It was during her absence that the accident happened, not in Sta. Mesa but in my penthouse, where, as I already mentioned, I enjoyed my sensual distractions.

She was Spanish, from Madrid, and had won some beauty contest there. As it often happened, I always tested each piece of merchandise before I passed it on to my avid customers. She was on a tourist visa and even before she left Madrid, she already knew she had a lot of entertaining to do in Manila. No riffraff certainly, but the richest, the suavest men in town and in a manner most discreet and refined in keeping with her status as a beauty queen. And even if she had not been, the same decorum was always observed.

Luisita—she was nineteen. Her father clerked in a bank and her mother was a schoolteacher. There were eight of them in the family, and four were girls. She was the oldest of the girls and, according to my man who recruited her, the prettiest. Eight in the family—so I can easily imagine how much she wanted a better life.

In the first two days after she arrived, I escorted her to a reception where, I am sure, she attracted a lot of attention. I knew then that she could even, as had happened, end up marrying into one of the mestizo families that craved strengthened racial ties with the old country. She had passed the physical examinations—a little bit embarrassing for her, but after what had happened to me, I did not take any chances.

From the very start, I told her she could get married in Manila if that was what she wanted, and I need not parade her around, but she demurred. Nothing like Madrid, she said. She would go back to be a model. This was a vacation and nothing more, so she decided she would make the most of it.

My man billeted her at the Manila Hotel but, tonight, and all the days that I wanted her, she would be with me. From the Club, we went to the penthouse. Even while we were still dining, I could already imagine how the evening would be. At fifty, I had taken good care of myself and was healthy and fit; I had even quite forgotten the dread disease I had contracted in my youth and the possibility that something in me had been damaged, an internal organ, my brain perhaps? There was one sure havoc it had wrought on me—I was no longer capable of procreation but, thank God, I was not rendered impotent.

Martial law was well into its seventh year. But even in those days that curfew was imposed, the palace had given me a special pass to travel anywhere at any time I pleased. As a procurer—I would never permit anyone to call me that!—I had the gratitude of this nation's highest officials.

At the time, the Leader had already grabbed the properties of his political enemies and jailed almost all of them. As I said, I had known the man since his earliest days in Congress, and we had become friends, though not too close. There was always the possibility that he would also take over my Philippine properties—I had seen, long before he came to power, the necessity of diversifying abroad, of developing ties elsewhere. Had he grabbed what I owned, he would be sending the wrong signals to the international business community, the Americans most of all, the Japanese, the Germans. How little Filipino entrepreneurs understood the necessity of such connections!

I read the Leader early enough, too. His heroic posturing,

his military cant betrayed his lack of physical courage, but he had managed his life very well, his marriage, his alliances. The flaw in the man was hubris, intoxicating and illusionary; he believed he could get away with anything merely because he was able at the start to wriggle out of a death sentence.

What a successful entrepreneur he would have been if he had merely paid attention to getting rich; but he personified unbridled conceit and every man should beware of this. Perhaps I cultivated that conceit, too.

As for Delfin's idol, Nojok's incarceration must have been regarded by my son with some pride, justifying his faith in the man. The income of the law office suffered, but not once did Delfin come to me for help. I continued sending him money—not as much as I wanted to, knowing he did not use it himself. He never acknowledged it or thanked me.

I inquired from my people in San Quentin if Delfin's relatives were doing well. They had my money, but not the others, the former tenants who were given title to the land they tilled. They could not keep up with the amortization. I expected this. But not what they did afterward—they sold the land and, soon enough, they were tenants again. I hope this was not lost on Delfin.

I was talking about the accident that crippled me, that forced me to look at my own mortality, that in spite of the means at my command, my existence on this earth is transitory and brief. But first, let me dispel the rumors that have spread about my accident, stories hallowed by gossip that I did not exactly regard as derogatory for they tend to confirm my machismo. It is not true that I suffered a stroke while being on top—that is, while performing man's most delectable function. Nothing of that sort at all, as the doctors at the Makati Center will readily confirm, as my penthouse staff will also relate. The accident was caused by my carelessness, my anxiety perhaps, although no woman can make me anxious now at this age.

It was not even nine in the evening. I was getting bored with Luisita's account of her middle-class Madrid life. I wanted the dinner and the dull conversation to be done with, so we hurried to the penthouse. We had showered together, but I urged her to finish first so that she could proceed to the bedroom, ready herself for my grand entrance.

I took my time—I always do—and had already rubbed myself dry. Then, as I stepped out of the tub, I was propelled into the air and my last sensation before I blacked out was a tremendous and painful whack on the back of my head as it hit the rim of the bathtub. I had stepped on the cake of soap that had slipped from the edge of the tub where Luisita had carelessly placed it.

When I regained consciousness, it was as if I had awakened from a deep stupor, a sleep from which I was not rested. I was disoriented, my senses seemed awry and malfunctioning, and I could hardly recall what had transpired. I closed my eyes quickly and tried to put some order to my thinking, and it came with a sharp twinge of regret that I was unable to savor what Luisita had to offer. Luisita! I was in a suite at the Medical Center. My head, like my whole body, felt very light. I opened my eyes again; I was surrounded by half a dozen men in white—all doctors. They seemed very serious, unsmiling. I tried to raise my arm in a gesture, but it refused to move. My other arm was nerveless, too, and so were my legs. It was then that I realized I was paralyzed. I screamed, heard the animal sound that escaped from me. I could talk, I could smell the sharp, peculiar odor of the hospital, I could hear their low conversation. They told me that I had been in a coma for three days, that my head wound required five stitches and that I had suffered brain damage.

I was now convinced I was possessed by some malignant and inexorable spell cast no less by my dear Severina before she died. I was defenseless against that dark, unseen power that she wielded; surely, she must have hated me for having abandoned her. Who was the harbinger of her hatred? Could it be Delfin? But my son, my son—my flesh is his flesh and I love him—I realized this from my own scabrous depths, within the knotted tangle of my own emotions. Surely, he could not be the instrument. The amulet that dangled from his neck, did it really protect him, and from whom? Certainly not from me who loved him, who wished for him the endless plenitude of the earth!

Corito came and sat on my bed. She was crying, but not only over what had happened to me. "Carling," she sobbed, "Angie has left San Francisco—and the maid does not know where she went. She has disappeared and I don't know where to find her."

Here I was, a useless cripple, and my Angela gone. There was only one person she would go to, but Corito was too distressed to think properly.

"Go see Delfin," I said. I could speak clearly without slurring the words.

Of course, I was right. Angela had heard of my accident but did not realize it was very serious. She immediately came to see me.

She brought to my arid suite the effulgence of her youth, her beauty. My Angela, her face flushed, happy and sad all at once. Her mother was not with her; obviously, they had already seen one another.

"Forgive me, Tito," she said, bending over to kiss me. She was holding my hand, but I could feel none of the warmth, the softness of her hand. "I am now living with Delf."

"In that tiny apartment?"

"Ummm." She smiled, the corners of her mouth crinkling. Again, the impish smile. "He loves me, Tito. The day before Mama and I left, I seduced him. I am pregnant and very happy."

My Angela happy! I didn't know that tears had gathered in my eyes and were rolling down my cheeks. She hastily wiped them off, then bent over and kissed me again.

Corito had flown in six specialists from the United States and they examined me thoroughly. If it was necessary for me to fly to the United States, I would charter a jet.

But they all said it was not necessary. I was already getting all the medical care I needed, and therapy, too. The possibility of my regaining mobility was remote.

I shouted at them, "Tell me the truth!" And that is what they said. "The truth." Complications, too, could easily develop. Will I die soon? They did not speak—in my condition, I was already dead.

I asked for Angela again and, when she came, I told her my remaining days were few. "I want to see you and Delfin. As soon as possible. This evening, if you can bring him here."

▨

So there they were, Jake, my chief counsel, Delfin and Angela. Delfin had aged in the year that I had not seen him. I longed to embrace him, if only these wretched arms could reach out. He was in a barong—he had a hearing in court that afternoon. His face was unsmiling, grim, as he looked at me.

Was he sad, too?

Jake and I were classmates at the Ateneo; he knew some of my secrets in business but not my personal ones. Like I said, I never let anyone get very close to me. I had asked him to bring a lot of things and his briefcase bulged with them.

"Jake," I told him, "first my will. Read it."

Jake was in college dramatics and had a theatrical manner. He started clearly, "Being of sound mind . . ."

"The date, Jake," I interrupted him. "The date."

He glanced at it and read it.

I could, at least, turn my head. I faced Delfin. "So you see,

Delfin. Do you remember the day? It was when you enrolled in law school, *hijo*. That early, I had already made my will—the third time it was changed. And the last time . . ."

I asked Jake about my liabilities, the liquidity of my assets. He had brought along the annual statement prepared by my accountants. I was again confirmed; I was, indeed, very, very rich! He continued reading my will.

Corito would get what remained of the hacienda and all the properties our parents had left. But she had also appended her own will to mine, that those properties would pass on to Angela—most of it, except a little for a couple of nieces whom she liked. And all of mine would go to Delfin and to Angela, with provisions for a couple of pretty cousins who had been particularly good to me, and for people like Jake, who had served me well. A short will, not more than five pages. I asked Jake to leave when he was through.

All the while, Delfin had stood there, silent, erect like a marble pillar.

"I warned you about misfits being the offsprings of first cousins marrying," I told him. How could I ever tell them the truth? And would it really matter now?

My mind was filled with those awful clichés. "Money—wealth, when was it ever bad? It all depends on how it is used. The acquisition, well, who would now accuse the Rockefellers, the Morgans of the United States—those robber barons as they were called? It was they who made America."

"No do-gooding can ever erase history, sir."

"But even do-gooding is never enough. What happened to those tenants in the hacienda who were given land? I did that to please you—and also to teach you a lesson. They sold their farms, became tenants again!"

He was silent, then he said, "Giving them land isn't enough. Rural credit, farm management training—they should have these, too."

"And you expected me to do these?" I shouted, but what

came out was a squeak. "That is the function of government, not me!"

A most awkward silence. I was speaking from the depths of my being, shredding my heart, exposing my very nerves. "Severina—it was so long ago and I was just a teenager. What did I really know about love? But looking back, remembering how I missed her after she had gone, I am now sure that I loved her in my own fashion, young as I was. Why did she not write to me? Tell me about you? I would have come to see her, to hold you. Please, I implore you, believe that. Not everything was my fault. When you came, you cannot know how sincerely, lovingly, I welcomed you. I didn't ask you for any proof. One look at you and everyone will say, You are a chip off the old block. Do you understand that expression? It is very dated . . ."

Delfin nodded, a wry smile on his face at last.

"You are very proud, *hijo*. I appreciate that. So am I. But every so often, aware as I am of my tremendous strength, I let the weak be. I live in a jungle—we all do—but what profit does it give us to rampage and trample the weak? Better to use them. Look at my companies. My tenants, my workers, get much, much more than the minimum wage, more privileges than those toiling in those Chinese sweatshops, those creaky establishments owned by the Indios. There is Spanish blood in you—mine. Look at all the successful businesses and organizations in this country. They are all Spanish mestizo, or Chinese mestizo—not Indio. My father and my grandfather believed that the Indio is inferior, that his brain is not big enough for creativity or management. It is us, mestizos, with our mixed blood, who will bring this nation up from the dung heap. You have a big role to play, not just as my son but as a Filipino, for that is what the term originally meant—the Spaniards who were born here—"

He interrupted me loudly. "Sir, I will not stand for this racist nonsense!"

"But it is the truth," I shouted, this time realizing that my voice was no longer a squeak but what it had always been, strong, clear, imperial. "The truth! Look at your guru, the man you idolize. Nojok is mestizo, too!"

"He is Filipino," he said with conviction, his eyes blazing.

"Enough of this," I said. "I have made my point. Now, you and Angela—if you really love her, you will not want her to live as harshly as you are living. You will want her to have some comfort. You don't even have a maid!"

"She told me she wouldn't mind," he said meekly. I had touched a raw nerve. I was going to make the most of it.

"Not mind! Of course she told you that; she loves you. I love Angela, too, like she was my very own. I do not think you really love her, *hijo*."

"You are very wrong, sir," he replied quickly. "I do. I do!" Then he turned away and faced the window. From my top-floor suite, the new city of Makati spread below. From where I lay, helpless, immobile, I could see my own office building, a tower of gleaming glass in the near distance, my penthouse hidden from view.

Luisita, she had caused all this. No, it was not my libido. My sins inexorably coming again to visit me. My staff had sent her to her hotel before the ambulance came. Then immediately the following morning, she left for Hong Kong and home. She was traumatized by what had happened, but the hefty sum given her must have salved her somewhat.

When Delfin turned to me again, his eyes had misted. "Angela told you that she seduced me. That is not true at all, sir. Since she was young, I had watched her, seen her grow, so sensitive, so frail. I thought I would protect her. With all that beauty, I did not want her to be like my mother—bearing an illegitimate child. But now . . ."

"Marry her," I said. "Neither Corito nor I will stand in the way. But in heaven's name, don't let her suffer. Let her live with some comfort at least. I looked at her hands—they were bruised . . ."

"I told her not to wash my clothes . . ."

"But she did it just the same. Yes, a woman in love is capable of abnegation. But she is pregnant now and she needs all the care in the world, sickly as she is."

He avoided my gaze. I was getting to him at last.

"I love you both," I said. "Had I known about you then, I am sure I would have come to claim you, to give your mother some honor. I am stubborn, too. I would have challenged my parents like you are challenging me now. But I would never have hated my parents, my father most of all, not so much for what they left me but because I grew up with their love. Ah, Severina, forgive me. It was not all my fault. Did you raise our son to be proud? He is brilliant, but did you raise him to hate me, too?"

Emotions I couldn't control came surging, waves as high as mountains collapsing on me. Paralyzed as I was, I could feel my chest tightening, making it difficult for me to utter another word. I was sobbing like a child, I know, but did not know tears were rolling down my cheeks.

"Please, sir, believe me. Mother . . . she never told me to hate you. Never!"

"*Hijo*," I said between sobs that were wrenched from me like tendons stripped off my bones. "When are you going to stop calling me 'sir'? When Americans say 'sir' they do it to put some distance between them and those they address as sir. Call me anything, *hijo*, anything but 'sir.'"

It was then that he came to me, took a handkerchief from his pocket and, bending over me, wiped the tears on my cheeks. My son, my son, in this first act of kindness, and all the more did this feeling of sadness, diluted now with some joy, sweep over me again and again, and it would seem that my sorrow could not be contained anymore, till my whole body, inert and unfeeling, was squeezed dry of it.

But as he leaned over, the amulet he had always worn on his neck slid out of his shirt. Was it an uncanny trick of light? Or my eyes, diseased as they may already be, playing a shocking trick on me? It dangled close, almost touching my face, taunting and mocking me, no longer hematein. It had changed color. Now, it was a shiny, even glittering, triangle of the deepest black.

✠

Two decorations in one day! This morning, after my ablutions, the Spanish ambassador came and presented me with Spain's highest decoration, "The Grand Cross of Isabella." Now it's out. I have Spanish citizenship, too! He gave a short speech that my loyal staff applauded gustily. Then he bent over and hung around my neck this gold medallion with a thick yellow sash. It was a little early for Dom Perignon but, just the same, it was passed around and a joyous mood suffused my suite. In the late afternoon, the Leader himself came and also made a short sweet speech and then he hung on my neck another gold medallion, "The Order of Lapu-lapu," the highest honor the government can bestow on one of its citizens.

I knew it—the decorations were meant to be my epitaph. And there was no Angela, no Corito, no Delfin to witness my triumph—and my passing.

I suddenly remembered that unique interview in *Esquire* some years back with Groucho Marx when, like me, in his senility, he was being decorated by foreign governments. The interviewer had asked him for a comment on his latest decoration from the French government and the old rascal, without a second thought, said, "I'll give them all up for just one erection!" End of interview.

Not me, not me. I'd give them all up for two erections!

This was what brightened my mind and I started laughing uproariously till I realized the impossibility of it all. The sluices of sadness opened and I began to weep, then sob just as loudly. The Leader came to me, patted me on the shoulder. He drew a handkerchief from his pocket and started to wipe my cheeks. I cried out, "No, Mr. President. No!"

Perhaps he thought I was being modest, that I didn't want that presidential attention. That was not the reason. His handkerchief smelled! Really smelled!

✖

Dying and crippled as I am, I had thought I could now be at peace with myself, with the demons that have hounded me, with my sister, in spite of her lascivious appetites—and my dear children.

I had carefully laid down my succession; my trusted lieutenants like Jake would see to that. Although I am now nailed to this wheelchair, they can move me about. Two special vans, like ambulances with special ramps to ease me down or clamp me in place beside the driver's seat, enable me to move about, to see the edifices I have built, the multitude that do my bidding. Wherever I go, my people cheer me, indomitable in spirit—that is what they think I am. They do not see the anxieties that canker me, corrode and slowly destroy me.

Are they telling me the truth when I question them about the viability of their enterprises? Can I trust them really as I trusted them once? I rant and shout—I think I do—and they simply smile and nod in acquiescence, or is it obeisance? Even Jake, without whom I could not operate, is that contempt in his bland mestizo face? Or is it pity?

"Jake!" I snarl at him. "Would you jump into a vat of boiling oil if I told you to?"

He grins. It is an old joke between us. "I will push you in first, then follow—" he repeats the scripted reply and laughs. He will push me in first, and that's that, of this I am now sure. To him will go so much of the fortune I have built; he is very clever; will he be able to go around my will? To cheat Delfin and Angela of their legacy? I am almost sure he would be capable—he had done so many things with me in the past that would land us both in jail if he blabbered. I do not think I can trust him anymore.

Delfin should now be constantly by my side, but he does not come to see me. Has Jake ringed me with an insurmountable wall of steel? That bastard son, that bastard son, after all that I have done for him! And my Angela, my precious Angela, where is she? That little bitch, that pretty little bitch, she, too, has forsaken me. And my sister, Corito, you blasted whore! It is all your fault!

The world around me becomes gray, then black, and I close my eyes as tightly as I can, and the images that form in the hollow of my brain, fragmented and overlapping one another, are rough-edged slabs of gold, now silver, now ebony, and then laser flashes of deep red piercing my soul and I know I am again about to be seized by panic.

I dare not open my eyes. I cry out, "Severina, Severina, stop it! Lift this curse you have damned me with. I do not deserve it. Have I not been mortified enough? Have I not pleaded with you long enough? Forgive me, Severina. Forgive me!"

But it cannot be. I see everything I have built slowly collapse like sand castles lapped by the waves. I open anxiously my pyxis of memories but find nothing of value there. I see instead the world's end coming, blacker than night, and all I can do is wait.

When was the last time I saw Delfin? Corito? They are nowhere now. And my Angela, where is she? The last time I saw her—how can I forget it? I had thought that in my hapless condition I would grieve no more, that I would no longer regret my inability to move and to act. She had come to me so pale and distraught, those big brown eyes languid with sorrow, with anger, and whatever else was deeply troubling her. "Oh, Tito," she wailed. "Is it true? Is it true?"

I waited for her to utter the words, the final acknowledgment of what she truly was and I as well.

"They—" then she broke down and cried. She flung herself upon me, and though I could not embrace her I could feel her shudder on my nerveless body as sobs were torn out of her.

"What is it Angela, *hija*?" I asked in a voice that quavered.

She went on crying. Briefly, she was aware of the four nurses on duty and, through her tears, she told them to leave, that she wanted to be alone with me. When they did not move, I barked at them, "Out! Out!"

We were finally alone. Between sobs, she told me how she had found Corito and Delfin in a sexual embrace in their apartment, how Corito had told her that she and Delfin could not get married because they were brother and sister.

"Is it true, Tito?" She turned to me, her large eyes gazing, probing deep into me.

I had to look away and couldn't speak.

She half rose and embraced me, kissed me on the cheek, the tears streaming down her cheeks, and all the while she was mumbling, "Oh, Tito. Oh, Tito. But you were always a father to me. Yet I find it so difficult now to call you Papa. Oh, Tito, thank you just the same for having been so good to me . . ." Then she stood up, smiled at me through her tears and slowly walked to the door.

"Angela," I called in my raspy, croaking voice, "Angela! It was not my fault! It's fate—fate, believe me, dearest! And those infernal witches. *Brujas!*"

But I do not think she heard or cared.

GLOSSARY

accesorias	Apartments; literally, "outbuildings" (Sp.). Word used widely until the 1950s.
bangus	Milkfish.
chitcharon	Fried pork skin (Sp.).
cuedao	Filipinized variation of *cuidado*, "be careful" or "beware" (Sp.).
dokar	Two-wheeled horse-drawn carriage; word used only during World War II.
encargado	Person in charge; administrator of a plantation (Sp.).
ganta	Measure of grain; term no longer used, as grain is measured in kilos.
hacendero	Landlord; owner of a big plot of land, from *hacienda* (Sp.).
Huks	Communist-led revolutionary group that fought for agrarian reform in the Philippines after World War II; it grew out of an anti-Japanese resistance movement in Luzon during the war.
ilustrados	The first Filipinos, usually of means, who studied in Europe (beginning in the 1880s) in order to become "enlightened"; literally, "learned" or "well-informed" (Sp.).

jusi barong   A loose-fitting, long-sleeved man's shirt—
the national dress of the Philippines—made
from fine, sheer fabric, often embroidered on
the collar and facing.

kundiman   A sad folk song, usually Tagalog.

merienda   Afternoon snack (Sp.).

ningas cogon   Famous Filipino expression denoting enthu-
siasm that dies quickly, like cogon grass that
burns quickly in the dry season.

poulownia   A very expensive rare wood used for furniture.

ABOUT THE AUTHOR

With the publication of *Three Filipino Women* by Random House in 1992, the work of F. Sionil José began appearing in the United States. He is one of the major literary voices of Asia and the Pacific, but (after encouragement by Malcolm Cowley and others) his novels and stories are only now gradually being published in the country that figures in much of his work as both a shadow and yet a very real presence.

José (widely known as "Frankie") runs a leading bookshop in Manila, was the founding president of the Philippines PEN Center, publishes the journal *Solidarity,* and is best known for the five novels comprising the highly regarded *Rosales Saga* (*Po-On; Tree; My Brother, My Executioner; The Pretenders;* and *Mass*), which are being prepared for publication in America. He is widely published around the world and travels steadily.

F. SIONIL JOSÉ BY DONG KINGMAN

ABOUT THE TYPE

This book was set in Galliard, a typeface designed by Matthew Carter for the Merganthaler Linotype Company in 1978. Galliard is based on the sixteenth-century typefaces of Robert Granjon.